Advance Praise for *Apology Accepted*:

Wood's third book in the Colbie Colleen suspense fiction series doesn't disappoint! Well-written and an easy read, I couldn't wait to pick it up after work—or, before work!

—W.D. Samuels

As an author, I'm always thrilled when I find a writer who knows how to build suspense with a few red herrings thrown in to keep the reader honest—Wood is a master!

—Barrett E. McKinnon, Author
The Manufactured Messiah

Woods is a 5-star author! Her Colbie Colleen series is suitable for readers of all ages, and I always find myself looking forward to her next book. Do yourself a favor, and get to know Colbie Colleen—you won't be disappointed!

—Pauline Marr

If you love reading Patterson, Grafton, or any other suspense fiction author, you'll thoroughly enjoy Wood's third book, Apology Accepted. Beautifully crafted, the author transports readers into a world of intrigue and intuition where things are seldom as they seem. Such a fun read!

—M. Marshall

Apology Accepted

Apology Accepted

a Colbie Colleen suspense fiction novel

Faith Wood

Double Your Faith Productions
Vernon, British Columbia, Canada

ISBN: 978-1545304198

ISBN: 154530419X

Printed in the United States of America

DEDICATION

"Always remember you are braver than you believe, stronger than you seem, and smarter than you think."

—Christopher Robin

Sometimes the most significant apology of our lives should be to ourselves for doubting our own abilities . . .

Apology Accepted!

—Faith Wood

CHAPTER ONE

From her open door, Colbie watched Tammy place items from her desk in several, small cardboard boxes, then tape them carefully on the sides and top. She couldn't be sure, but she thought she heard a sniffle or two. *Maybe it's for the best*, Colbie thought. *She'll be happy, and I can always get another assistant . . . just not as good.*

The truth was changes in her life were coming at exactly the right time, although she refused to admit it three months earlier. Since returning from South Africa, Colbie realized a spike in her business as well as her relationship with Brian, and, for two years, they lived the life of her dreams. Granted, there wasn't a picket fence, but living in the country outside of Boston was a pretty good start. But, when Tammy broke the news she was getting married and moving to Florida—well, things started happening quicker than Colbie imagined.

For the first time in their lives, money wasn't a consideration. After breaking the art theft case in London and Cape Town, she became a name on everyone's lips—especially those within law enforcement. By the time she and Brian landed on American soil, clients were lined up at the door, and she had her choice of cases. Although it may seem weird to some, Colbie didn't prefer cases that might end up in the limelight—no, as nice as the recognition was, she preferred to fly under the radar. Doing so was better for her, better for Brian, and better for her intuitive mind.

Lost in thought, she didn't hear Tammy until she knocked twice. "I'm ready . . ."

Colbie dreaded the next few minutes as she stood, approaching her assistant. Saying goodbye spiked such raw emotion, she feared she wouldn't get through it gracefully. "I see that—I'll help you carry stuff to your car . . ."

Tammy smiled. "Not necessary—Gary's going to be here in a few, and we can get everything between the two of us."

"It's not going to be the same, you know . . ."

"Life won't be the same for me, either—but, who would have thought I'd find the perfect guy for me and my kid?" Tammy cocked her head as she looked at her soon to be former boss. "But, what about you?"

"Me? What about me?" Colbie grinned at the slender, young woman. "I'll be just fine—although, I'll miss you. You were with me from the beginning, and it will be weird to walk in here Monday morning without seeing you at your desk . . ."

Tammy turned as the office door opened and closed. "Hey! I'm ready to go—give me a sec?"

Gary grinned and nodded, picked up three boxes at

once, and headed out the door. "I'll be back for the rest . . ."

Tammy and Colbie stood in silence, neither having the courage nor desire to say goodbye.

"So—how about if I check in after we settle in Florida? We leave tomorrow, so I'll be available after next week . . ."

"Sounds perfect—travel safely, and I'll try not to bug you when I can't find something!"

A quick hug later and a brief last look at her outer office, Tammy was out the door to a new life. As it closed softly, Colbie's tears finally spilled, laying bare feelings for no one to see. Over the past year, she realized something was changing within her, and dealing with tangled emotions became a daily battle. She no longer felt her strength and courage would always be there for her and, when working cases, she felt emotions surge instead of calculated intellect—not the best situation.

By the time lights were flickering on in city buildings, Colbie packed her laptop in her favorite messenger bag. Ready to tackle the weekend, her fingertips lingered on the light switch as she briefly glanced at Tammy's desk.

Empty.

CHAPTER TWO

"I know—it's going to be different without her. But, if there's one thing I know about you, it's your ability to make the best of any situation." Brian paused as he handed Colbie a glass of merlot. "Have you started looking for her replacement yet?"

Colbie accepted the goblet, placing it on the table between them. "That's just it—I put off hiring because I didn't want to deal with it . . ."

"Ah—I get it. But, I have to say that doesn't sound like the Colbie Colleen I know—you always tackle everything head on . . ." He glanced at her as he handed her a warm wedge of melting brie cheese on a small, rustic board. "Is everything okay?"

Colbie picked up a water cracker, smearing it with the

gooey delight, taking her time before answering. "Well—I have been thinking about something . . ."

Brian shifted in his chair so he would have a good view of her. "I'm all ears—what's on your mind?"

Colbie swallowed her bite of cracker, then took a sip of wine. "What do you think about moving back home?" She hesitated, letting her intuition guide her. "I got a call . . ."

"A call? From whom?" Ever since she knew him, Brian was never one to conceal his feelings with a deadpan face, and it was clear he wasn't expecting a bombshell. "You mean back to the West Coast?"

"Well—around there . . ."

Brian was silent for a moment, thinking about the possibility of picking up and moving. "So—who called?"

"You're never going to believe this—Nicole Remington." She waited for him to erupt.

"Nicole Remington? What the hell did she want?"

Colbie watched Brian's face narrow into something dark just thinking about the woman who held him captive years ago. "I know—I couldn't believe it, either. But, before you go off the deep end, remember she didn't have much choice—and, she paid the price for her part in the kidnapping . . ."

Brian fumed as he recalled time lost. "I hardly think that qualifies her to have access to you—or, me. So—what did she want?"

Another pause. "She wants to hire me . . ."

"Hire you? For what?"

"She says it's about a murder . . ." Colbie took another

sip. She could tell Brian was pissed just thinking about Remington—and, she couldn't blame him. Asking him to return to the place where he endured the worst years of his life wasn't an easy thing to do. And, if he weren't interested, that was fine. She'd turn down the case, and move on to something else.

"Who's murder?"

Colbie leveled her eyes on the man sitting next to her. "Her brother . . ."

Brian stiffened, trying to understand. "Why you? There are a million investigators out there—why can't she call one of them?"

Colbie ignored the veiled insult. "That's what I asked her—she said I'm the only one who can get to the bottom of what happened to him . . ." She had to admit, Remington had a point—because of her involvement with Brian's kidnapping, she knew of Colbie's abilities firsthand.

Brian swished what was left of the wine in his glass, thinking about the possibilities—and, consequences. It took him a long time to recover, and he wasn't sure he had the guts to face it again. "Tell me what you know . . ."

"Well—I don't know much because I only spoke to her last week. With Tammy's leaving, I didn't give it much thought until I was on my way home tonight." Colbie paused, looking directly at Brian. "And, believe me, I'm not taking Remington's offer lightly—you're my first concern and, if you don't think it's a good idea, I completely understand. There are plenty of cases I can consider . . ."

Brian knew that was true—but, he also knew there must be something about Remington's case that intrigued her. For her to consider working with that bitch meant something, and he had to keep that in mind.

"How did her brother die? And, who the hell is he? Does anyone even care he's dead?" He knew his words were harsh, but he didn't care. "Not only that, how the hell can Nicole Remington afford you? That bitch has a lot of nerve, if you ask me! And, I don't know how you can think about working for her . . ." He paused, Nicole Remington's face fresh in his mind. "It's not right . . ."

Colbie waited until Brian's white-knuckled grip on the arm of his chair relaxed a bit. "Interestingly, money was the first thing we talked about—she didn't want to explain anything about the case until I was comfortable with the idea she can pay. Turns out her family was firmly rooted in the banking business—the Champagnes, if I remember correctly.

"Champagne? Are you kidding?"

Colbie grinned. "I know—I couldn't believe it, either. But, when I was about twenty, there was a kid in my class whose last name was Champagne." Colbie paused, thinking about the scrawny kid who sat in front of her in Abnormal Psych. "I thought it was weird then, too . . ."

Brian couldn't help but laugh! "Okay—this Champagne guy. What did he do to get himself offed?"

"That's the thing—no one has a clue. According to Remington, he was the nicest guy in the world—his employees and family loved him and, at first glance, he didn't have any enemies . . ."

"In banking? No enemies? Sorry—I'm not buyin' it . . ."

"Nor do I—and, Remington isn't falling for it. She says cops haven't come up with anything, and she thinks her brother's murder will go cold if something isn't done soon."

Brian drained his glass, his face set with percolating anger. "When do you have to let her know?"

"I told her I had to talk to you first, and I'd get back with her by the end of the week . . ."

"Today's Friday . . ."

Colbie was silent as she thought about what she was asking of him. "I know—I wasn't sure if I should even bring it up with you . . ."

"So—what are you thinking? What do you think about working for Remington?"

Colbie drew a long breath before answering. "Good question—as I listened to Remington's voice on the phone, my radar was pinging, and I got the feeling she's different somehow. Still, even if she has changed, that will never trump what she did to you . . ."

"So—you're willing to consider it?"

"Are you?"

Brian grew quiet, looking at the woman beside him. Since they returned from Cape Town, their relationship flourished, and he couldn't remember a happier two years. And, even though he didn't understand them, he believed in Colbie's intuitive abilities. He saw them work, and he couldn't dispel her accuracy.

But, there was something else to consider—as much as he loathed the idea of seeing Remington's face again, his years of therapy taught him in order to regain control over his life, he must confront his kidnapping head on. *Maybe,* he thought, *that means returning to ground zero—maybe it is time to go home . . .*

He glanced at Colbie. "Maybe—but why did you ask me how I felt about moving? Just because you have a case on the West Coast doesn't mean we have to move there . . ." He hesitated as if trying to figure something out. "Does it?"

Colbie shook her head. "No—it doesn't mean we have to move. But, I'm not going to lie—life on the Eastern Seaboard doesn't agree with me, and I realize I miss my roots. Maybe I'm a West Coast person—I don't know." She paused, then offered an idea germinating for the last couple of days. "There isn't any reason we can't close up shop here, and head west for the duration of the Remington case . . ." She glanced at Brian. "That's if we decide to accept it . . ."

"We?"

"Hell, yes 'we'! If you think I'm working on my own for this case you're nuts!" Colbie noticed an uncertain flush creep from his neck to his forehead. In that moment she stopped, realizing what was at stake for her boyfriend. "But, as I said, if you're not up for it, then we stay right where we are . . ."

Brian rested his head on the back of the chair, thinking of all the things that could go wrong. He had a gut feeling returning to the city where he was kidnapped was a bad idea, but he couldn't point to one specific reason.

Until Colbie recognized it for him. "I understand if you're afraid to go back there—anyone would be apprehensive if they experienced what you did . . ."

He knew she was right—returning to the west scared the hell out of him, and there was a possibility he would undo all of his progress during the last two years. "Not gonna lie—the idea scares the crap out of me . . ."

"I know—I see it in your face . . ."

Brian fell silent, then scooped up the last of the cheese

on a corner of a cracker, cramming it in his mouth. "Then, again—why not? I think working with Dr. Carpenter for the last couple of years has done some good and, even though it's a scary thought . . ."

Colbie waited as he worked through what he wanted to say.

". . . I think we should go for it. After all, Remington is the one who finally spilled her guts—if it weren't for her . . ."

Colbie couldn't have been more proud! How could she consider leaving him two years ago before she left for London and Cape Town? The difference in their relationship served as testament to the possibility of things changing—all it takes is work, and commitment. *Two years ago*, she thought as she fondly looked at the strong man who felt as if he could take on anything, *he would have shriveled at the mention of Nicole Remington's name. Now? I shriveled more than he did . . .*

CHAPTER THREE

C losing up shop without Tammy's help was more time consuming than she expected. Colbie notified past clients she was working on an extended case, and would be unavailable for several months. Referrals, however, were another story—she felt it rude to not at least consider a case if referred by a current or previous client. "Referrals are my bread and butter," she once said, always sticking to her belief. So, after a round of personal calls—with Brian's help—she managed to close her office and house and, by the time spring drifted into summer, both were winging their way to Bellingham—returning home.

Of course, before they left, Colbie had a strict conversation with Nicole Remington about what she expected from her new client. While she didn't want to set a negative precedent at the beginning of the case, she felt it necessary to make Remington aware of the ground rules.

Rule number one?

Never mention Brian's kidnapping.

As they landed, Colbie congratulated herself for having the smarts to tell Remington she didn't want her meeting them at the plane. Although Brian would undoubtedly have to lay eyes on Remington sometime during their investigation, she didn't want it to be on their first day back in the city. If she played her cards right, Brian could investigate leads that didn't involve Remington directly—Colbie would be the one to have conversations with Nicole.

Before leaving Boston, Colbie and Brian were on the same page—once on the ground in Seattle, they'd head north to Bellingham, check in at their hotel, grab a bite to eat, and tuck in for the evening. The following day they had appointments with a realtor to check out long-term rentals— from what Colbie knew about the Champagne murder case, it was a good bet it could last for a year. She, however, wasn't quite ready to make that long of a commitment.

As the plane taxied to a complete stop, Colbie stole a glance at Brian. *He doesn't seem upset*, she thought as she tried to gauge his emotions and feelings. He stared out the window as passengers grabbed their bags, waiting until they were the last two to disembark. She suspected he was gathering courage, but was delighted when he turned to her sporting a giant grin.

"What are we waiting for? Get your ass moving!" He laughed as he helped Colbie from her seat. "Pizza sound good?"

"Pizza sounds fabulous!"

****

One perk of being successful was the opportunity to enjoy the best accommodations—their hotel wasn't swanky, but it was better than rooms she could afford when they lived in outside the city several years prior, yet nothing like the rooms in London and Cape Town.

"Does it feel weird to be back?" Colbie kept a close eye on Brian in case he started to subliminally telegraph he was having a tough time with his circumstances.

He shook his head. "To be honest, it feels surreal—I didn't think I'd ever come back here. But, it's not as bad as I thought . . ."

Colbie stopped hanging up her clothes in the closet next to the bathroom and leaned against the wall, a fond smile on her lips. "You know—I wasn't sure how you'd react to returning home, but, somehow, you manage to deal with it. I'm not sure I could be so confident . . ."

"Confident?"

"At least it seems that way . . ." She smiled again, returning her attention to the clothes. "As soon as we decide on a place to live, we can unpack everything when we move in. But, until then . . ." Her voice trailed as she concentrated on what they really needed while they were in the hotel. With luck, they'd be there for no more than a week—but, from everything she heard, the short-term rental market was next to nil, and they'd be lucky to find something that suited them.

Brian propped his feet up on the coffee table. "What

time do we meet with the realtor?"

Colbie expected his question—ever since the kidnapping, Brian fixated on time. She often thought it was because he had nothing but time when he was held hostage, and it became a fixation then, too—only different.

"The realtor? Nine-thirty. After that, I have a face-to-face with Remington—the quicker we get started, the quicker we solve the case . . ." Colbie glanced at Brian without his noticing. "Of course, you don't need to be a part of that—I'll tell you everything when I get back . . ."

"Good—confidence aside, I'm pretty sure I'm not ready to see her face . . ."

She closed the closet door, grabbed her glasses from her purse, and plopped on the couch next to him. "Good—that's settled." Colbie thought for a moment. "What are your thoughts about this murder? I mean—for Nicole Remington to call me after all we've been through . . . well, I think there's more to this than a simple murder . . ."

Brian cocked an eyebrow. "Simple murder? Is that possible?"

Colbie grinned. "You know what I mean—for someone to knock off a big-name banker? That tells me it's either personal, or someone had a vendetta . . ."

"What's your gut?"

"My gut?" She thought for a moment before answering. "Vendetta . . ."

"That's what I think—personal would be too easy. Besides, if it were personal, I think the cops would have latched on to something by now . . ."

"Agreed—from what Nicole told me, there's something about this whole thing that's really slick . . ."

"Meaning?"

"The only thing the cops have—or, had—is a dead body. No prints of anyone but the vic, and Champagne was executed—double tapped."

Brian fiddled with the bag of peanuts he got on the plane, finally opening it with such force, several caromed off the small coffee table, landing on the floor several feet from the couch. "Oh, man . . ."

Colbie laughed, and fished a bag of cashews from her purse. "Here—I already had mine!" She tossed the package at him, watching as he picked up the errant nuts, then settled back on the couch. "So," she continued, "with such a clean hit, that tells me it was a professional job . . ."

"Has Remington given you anything to go on?"

"Not really—all I know is what she told me, and what I learned from my Internet research. The murder was in all the papers and on T.V. for several weeks, but, eventually, it became a back-page story."

Brian popped a handful of nuts in his mouth, chasing them with swig of soda. "So—other than working with local police, we're starting at square one. Right?"

"Exactly . . ."

"What do you need me to do? And, remember—this is my first time, so be gentle . . ."

Colbie leaned over, planting a smooch on his cheek. "I promise!"

Both were quiet as they thought about Nicole

Remington, the murder of her brother, and what was really going on. Colbie's gut told her—even without comprehensive information from Nicole—there was something more sinister at play. As often happened at the beginning of her cases, she couldn't put her finger on it, but, of one thing she was certain—Champagne's murder was targeted. Calculated.

And, cunning.

****

They stood in front of a small, craftsman house—grey, white trim, and brightly-colored flowers adorning the walkway leading to the front door. As Colbie and Brian considered its possibilities, Colbie's intuitive mind suddenly exploded, visions whipping in and out, and she barely had time to concentrate on any of them. But, two standing out were the fictional character, Heidi, and, two AK-47 weapons. *What the . . .? Those don't even go together!* Colbie barely heard the realtor as she droned on about the pros about the property—but, by the time they crossed the threshold into the front room, Colbie knew it was the house for them. She glanced at Brian, trying to assess if his reaction were the same and, when she saw his slight smile, she knew.

It was the perfect 'welcome home'.

****

Colbie couldn't help but think how different Nicole Remington's home was from when she first met her. Then, it was a comfortable, brownstone on a tree-lined street, tastefully decorated—the antithesis of what she noticed as she pulled into the long, horseshoe drive. *Business must be good*, Colbie thought, as she cut the engine and checked her makeup in the sun visor's mirror.

She swiped on fresh lip gloss, then took a moment to study her surroundings. The home bordered on palatial, its lawn perfectly manicured and, as Colbie noted everything about the front of the house, a vision of a smiling man formed in her mind. It was then she knew—the mansion wasn't Remington's.

It was Reginald Champagne's.

Before she reached the front door, Nicole Remington stepped onto the veranda, extending her hand. "Colbie— thank you for coming . . ."

Her welcome, Colbie noticed, wasn't one of greeting an old friend. As she accepted the handshake, it was clear the past few years hadn't been kind to Remington, and all the facial surgery in the world wasn't going to erase time and circumstances.

"Nicole . . ." Both women weren't quite sure of what to say.

After a moment's awkwardness, Nicole spoke first. "Please, come inside—it's hotter than usual for this time of year, and we'll be more comfortable . . ." That was true—late spring in the Northwest wasn't usually so warm. But, that year, drought conditions ruled, and Colbie looked forward to conducting their meeting in the comfort of air conditioning.

Remington led her to a sitting room just off the front entrance where a crystal pitcher filled with lemonade and ice was flanked by two crystal glasses on a silver tray. She motioned for Colbie to sit down. "I know this is awkward," she admitted as she filled the glasses. "We don't have a good history and, to be honest, I never thought I'd see you again—let alone need your services . . ."

Colbie accepted the glass, and took a sip. "Well, I have to admit, it was a shock when you called . . ." She sat back, focusing on her new client. Remington's hands trembled slightly as she poured the lemonade, making Colbie wonder if the tremors were due to nerves, a health issue, or something else. "But," she continued, "I think it's in both of our interests to put the past behind us as we work on your case . . ."

Nicole's shoulders sagged with relief. "Agreed—where do you want to start?"

"Well—I think we need to start with your family. The Champagnes. You told me a few things during our phone conversations, but I don't feel as if I have a good handle on who they are . . ."

Remington nodded. "I'm not so sure I have a good handle on them, either! But, as you may have guessed, we're sitting in the home of Reginald Champagne—world-class banker. My brother . . ."

"I confess I noticed it was different than the brownstone you had . . ."

"Very different—but, in order to help with expenses during my trial, the brownstone was the first to go. My brother was kind enough to offer his home to me when I got out . . ."

"A kind gesture—what else can you tell me about him?"

"Reggie was one of the nicest guys you'd ever want to meet. He went out of his way to help people, and he didn't have an enemy in the world . . ."

Colbie looked at her in disbelief. "He had one . . ."

Nicole sat back in her chair, tears welling. "Indeed—he had one . . ."

In that moment, Colbie knew Nicole Remington was a changed woman. How much changed, she didn't know—but, no longer was there a sense of panache, or joie de vivre. In spite of her attempt to fend off age, it haunted her eyes and the hollows of her cheeks.

Over the next hour, Remington recounted growing up in a wealthy family, one that traipsed from continent to continent when they were old enough to travel. Reginald— three years older than she—was the gregarious one and, while she relegated herself to the background, her brother made friends easily. In fact, it reminded Colbie of her relationship with her own brother . . .

According to Remington, as they entered high school and college, Reginald had already set his life's path—to follow in his father's footsteps. "It was his calling," Nicole told her. "He adored our father—when he died, Reggie was devastated. He was barely old enough to take Father's place at the bank, so he learned by trial and error . . ." She paused for a moment. "And, he earned a position of respect among his peers and colleagues within a few years . . ."

Colbie placed her glass on the serving tray. "Your father owned the bank?"

"Yes—with partners."

"Are any of them still living?"

"One—but he has his people take care of day-to-day business because of his age . . ."

"Name?" Colbie plucked her notepad and pen from her purse. Doing so was one thing that changed over the past several years—she no longer relied on wisps of paper to write down pertinent information.

"Orville—Orville Gartner . . ."

Colbie wrote down the name as Remington spelled it. "The bank—national or international?"

"International . . ."

That came as a surprise. "Countries?"

"Switzerland . . ."

Colbie sat up a little straighter. Switzerland? No wonder she had a vision of Heidi! She chuckled to herself—her visions came to her in symbols and, sometimes, she didn't understand. The Heidi vision, however, was suddenly clear.

By the time Remington stood as a signal to wind it up, Colbie's brain was maxed, and she couldn't wait to report back to Brian about how Nicole changed, as well as what she learned about the Champagne family. There were, however, a few things that didn't make sense—why were they into international banking instead efforts on their own soil? And—in Switzerland? The country known for secure banking procedures, as well as confidentiality?

That tidbit of information just made my job a whole lot harder . . .

CHAPTER FOUR

————— ❖ —————

B rian sat on the couch, laptop open, bottled water at his side. It was a long while since he truly researched anything, but, before Colbie left for her meeting with Remington, she asked him to find out everything he could about the Reginald Champagne family. "We need to have a strong foundation," she said. "Between what I learn today, as well as what you learn from the Internet, we'll have a good idea of who he was . . ."

As he suspected, the second he typed in Champagne's name, a series of articles, web pages, and affiliations popped up—most were professionally prepared, but there were a few sparking his interest. Then, social media—the pages of Facebook and Twitter were where he would find out what people truly felt about Champagne. Nope—there was nothing. Anywhere. No social media, whatsoever. *Odd*, he thought as he tried site after site—still, nothing. It was then he resorted to something Colbie tried to teach him years ago—when things were good between them the first time, and they looked forward to spending their lives together.

He closed his eyes, trying to access his intuitive mind, although he suspected he wouldn't see or feel anything. The truth was he only gave it a snowball's chance in hell of working—but, when he started to recognize a form taking shape, he had to admit it was a little creepy. *How does she do this all the time*, he wondered as he allowed visions to form and recede. Of course, he didn't have a clue about what he was seeing or doing, but he recorded the visions on his phone, anyway. He figured he could go over them with Colbie—that's if he decided to tell her he dipped his toes in a pool he barely understood.

Fifteen minutes passed before he began to lift from his meditation. Unsure of what to expect, he allowed a slow entry back into reality and, once he was sure he had a grip, he stopped recording.

He knew listening to his own voice about something so foreign to him was going to be weird, but, truthfully? He didn't care. Brian was determined to be an asset to Colbie's investigation, no matter how uncomfortable it made him feel.

He rewound the recorder on his phone, not sure if he wanted to listen, unsure about what he said during his meditative session—at least from that standpoint, it might be interesting.

Then he tapped play.

Within moments, he heard his voice—a little lower and softer than usual—talking about everything he saw in his mind's eye. An A-frame home—*maybe a cabin,* he thought as he listened. The vision slipped in and disappeared so fast, he didn't have time to get a good look at it, but it appeared to have snow on its roof.

As he listened, he tried to recall the visions in his mind. Why, he didn't know, but he was beginning to understand what Colbie was talking about when she described things she saw during her meditations—nothing was clear, and everything was left to interpretation. Unfortunately, he didn't have enough experience to know what he was looking at—to him, it could mean anything.

Listening to the recording jogged his memory, and he realized he didn't have a clear recollection of what he saw. Upon hearing his voice, however, the visions came alive in his mind, and he recoiled as he pictured the most vile— something dark. A motorcycle. Pools of blood. But what was really weird was he also heard laughter as the visions shattered into splintered shards. *Laughter? What the hell is that about?* Then, a man's angry voice . . .

He was about to rewind the recording to listen to it again when he heard the latch on the front door. "Hey! Anybody home?" Colbie dropped her purse on the foyer library table.

Brian quickly turned off the recording. "Here—in the den . . ."

Colbie grinned as she kicked off her shoes, placing them by the door. "Okay—I picked up takeout. I figured neither one of us would feel like cooking . . . we have enough on our plates!" She laughed at her own pun, knowing Brian would appreciate it.

He did. As she rounded the corner into the cozy den, he rolled his eyes to the heavens. "Nice—cheap, but nice . . ."

"I couldn't resist!" She laughed as she placed two Styrofoam containers on the table. "So, what did you find out?"

"The usual—but what really surprised me was there was absolutely zilch on social media about Reginald Champagne."

Colbie paused as she doled out servings of a Thai noodles and chicken. "None?"

"Nada . . ."

She sat back, thinking about why that would be—for someone so well-known across continents, there had to be gossip going on somewhere. "Did you check Remington? Is there anything on social media about her?"

Brian's face flushed as he took his first bite of noodles. "Dang! This stuff is spicy!"

Colbie laughed. "What a lightweight! When did you get to be so delicate?"

"Delicate, my ass! This stuff is hardcore!"

She waited until he wiped beads of sweat from his forehead. "Sorry—next time I'll keep your sensitivity in mind . . ." She paused, thinking about Brian's social media discovery. "So—what about Remington? Was there anything about her?"

"Mostly stuff about the trial—nothing recent. It's as if someone made a concerted effort to remove everything about the family . . ."

"But, why? How? How can anyone remove all content from the boards or websites?"

They sat in silence for a moment, thinking about how difficult that would be. Of course, a person can take down a social media page, but to locate nothing when he typed in Reginald Champagne's name—other than the professional B.S.?

That was unusual.

Colbie wasn't sure she should ask, but the direct

approach seemed best. "Was it difficult?"

"Was what difficult?"

"Reading about Remington. If you ever think . . ."

Brian turned to look at her. "If I ever think I can't handle investigating Remington? Is that what you were going to say?" There was an edge to his voice she hadn't heard for a long time.

"Yes—that's exactly what I was going to say. Get real, Brian—Nicole Remington caused you more grief than anyone deserves. If you react strongly to investigating her, you don't have to go through with it . . ." There was something about Brian's tone that concerned her. Was he putting on a brave face so she wouldn't think less of him? She wondered— everything was so good during the last couple of years, it seemed silly to think he may slip back into depression. That fact, however, was a real possibility.

"I'm okay—but, I do have something to tell you . . ."

Colbie sat up, noting a subtle change in him. "Shoot— what is it?"

Brian paused as he took a bite—a small bite. "I tried what you do . . ."

"What do you mean, 'what I do'?"

"Meditation . . ."

She wasn't sure what he was talking about. "You mean meditation to calm yourself?"

"No—meditation to see if I can see what you see . . ."

Colbie was stunned! "Visions?"

"Yep . . ."

She could tell he was uncomfortable—perhaps embarrassed by his admission. Slowly, a wide grin. "How did it go? Did you see anything? What was it like?"

Brian laughed—she was like a kid at Christmas! "Well—I didn't have a clue about what I was doing, so I'm laying that down as a qualifier right now!" He glanced at her—she looked as if she were hanging on his every word. "It took me awhile, but I finally saw something that didn't make any sense—one of those A-frames . . ."

"You mean like a cabin?"

"Yeah—like a Swiss chalet . . ."

Colbie nearly bolted from her seat! "A Swiss chalet?"

Brian nodded. "Yeah—the kind you see in a travel magazine . . ."

Colbie sat back, still wondering if she were hearing him correctly. "You're never going to believe this . . ."

He looked at her, eyebrows arched.

She shifted her body so she could look directly at him. "When I met with Remington this morning, she told me her brother was entrenched in Swiss banking . . ."

"What?" It was Brian's turn to sit back, wondering if her heard her right.

"I kid you not—when I heard that, I immediately knew that tidbit of information was going to make our jobs harder."

"Harder? Why?"

"Think about it—how are we going to investigate the

case when there's a good chance the answer lies five thousand miles away?"

"Good point . . ." He paused. "So—you think my vision of the A-frame represents Switzerland? Is that how it works?"

Colbie nodded. "No doubt about it—your first vision is already corroborated! I'm usually not that lucky . . ." She snuggled next to him on the couch, enjoying the warm feeling of synchronicity. For the first time in their relationship, he could relate to her on a level she never thought possible. "Did you see anything else?"

Brian fell silent, as if he were remembering something. "Then it got weird . . ."

"Weird how?"

"It was so dark—I saw a motorcycle. I have no idea what that means—and, pools of blood . . ."

Colbie sat quietly, trying to decipher what Brian just told her.

"There's something else . . ."

She looked at him, suddenly concerned. "What?"

"I recorded it . . ."

"You recorded it? How?"

"My phone—I switched on the recorder, then sat back on the couch. I spoke out loud, describing what I saw— which, as I listened to it, wasn't much . . ."

"Do you still have the recording?"

Brian gave her a squeeze. "Do you want to listen?"

After a swift poke to his ribs, she sat up. "You know I do!"

****

Twenty minutes later, Colbie stared at him, completely stunned at what she heard. His meditation was clear and succinct and, even though he wasn't sure of what he was seeing, he described each symbol in vivid detail.

"Weird, huh?" Brian felt slightly embarrassed, knowing he was a novice at such a thing.

"For you, yes—me? Not so much . . ."

"Do you have any idea of what the motorcycle means? Or, the pools of blood?"

Colbie thought for a moment, then nodded. "The motorcycle could mean travel—a vehicle to get someplace." She paused, thinking about the blood. "The blood? I'm not sure . . ." She focused her complete attention on him. "But, what I think it means may not be important, at all—they're your visions, and you may develop a totally different way of interpreting them. You know—specific to you . . ."

Brian wasn't sure what to think. It still creeped him out a little, but, as he listened to Colbie explain things, he didn't feel quite so weird. "Let me ask you something—will I always see things, or can I hear things, too?"

"You mean you heard things in your head during your meditation?"

Brian nodded.

"What did you hear?"

"A man's voice—an angry voice . . ."

"Did you recognize it?"

"No . . ."

Colbie stood, then paced the room slowly. "If you can, describe it . . ."

Brian watched her as he tried to recall the voice he heard in his head. "It was filled with rage—but, I heard laughter, too. The same voice—does that make sense?"

She stared at him. "Oh, yes—it makes a ton of sense!" She sat beside him again, closer than before. "Was the voice young or old?"

"Definitely a mature man's voice . . ."

Colbie thought in silence before she asked the most pertinent question. "What did it say?"

Brian leaned forward, tenting his fingers of both hands. "Get out . . ."

"Are you sure?" She reached over, placing her hand on his forearm. "You're sure that's what you heard?"

"No doubt about it . . ."

Colbie sat back, then focused on Brian. "What do you think it means?"

"Shouldn't I be asking you that?"

"Maybe, but something tells me you already know . . ."

He turned to look at her. "It was a warning . . ."

CHAPTER FIVE

There's a certain sound associated with cold, hard, steel—and, it's not good. As massive doors clanged behind her, Colbie wondered what the hell she was doing there. Was it necessary? What good would it do? There was nothing to gain, really, except for a possible misguided thrill of seeing the man who upended her life behind bars. Of course, she didn't tell Brian—he would have flipped if he knew she intended to surface the past.

A guard guided her to a small conference room equipped with two chipped, green metal chairs, and a sturdy table the size of a postage stamp. A small window—too small for anything except providing light—was well out of reach, standing high above the heads of anyone who had the displeasure of sitting beneath it.

"You have fifteen minutes," the guard advised.

"I understand . . ." Colbie took a seat, and crossed her legs. Clearly, he didn't have any idea of who she was, and he probably didn't care—he treated her like anyone else without a thought of her being an ex-cop.

He stood by the door as the prisoner entered, shackled and cuffed, head down, nodding to the guard escorting the inmate. Then told him not to exceed fifteen minutes and, within moments, he was gone, leaving the three of them to their silence. The guard ordered the prisoner to sit, then took his place against the wall directly behind the man in the orange jumpsuit, its color signifying a penchant for or possibility of violence.

Colbie's heart raced as she looked at him—his once jacked physique succumbed to the rigors of gravity, and she figured he must have gained at least thirty or forty pounds. His skin was pasty from too much time spent indoors, and a small bald patch was blooming at the back of his head. All in all, Sergeant Rifkin looked every bit the prisoner who had given up.

"I imagine you're surprised to see me," Colbie began, waiting for a response.

"Not really . . ." Rifkin's voice sounded the same, but there was an unfamiliar edge.

"Not really? Are you telling me you knew I would come see you?"

"Of course—eventually. It's who you are . . ."

"What's that supposed to mean?"

Rifkin sat back in his chair, hands still cuffed, feet still shackled. "Oh, please, Colbie—you know what I'm talking about. You're weak—oh, you think you exhibit inner strength by coming here, but the truth is, you're wrestling with something beyond your control . . ."

"And, what would that be?"

Rifkin chuckled, his voice more arrogant than she remembered. "The fact you had no clue about who I really am . . ."

Colbie sat, stunned. His words a slap in the face, she felt her stomach sink as she realized he was right. In that moment she also realized the reason for her visiting him was to somehow forgive herself for not seeing the truth. She took him into her confidence. She allowed him to mentor her. She looked to him for guidance. How could she have been so wrong? How could he know she never forgave herself for not realizing the man she considered a friend was as dark as the devil's closet?

Rifkin laughed aloud as he recognized the self-degrading look on his former officer's face. "Do you have a mirror, Colbie?" He didn't wait for an answer. "If so, I suggest you take a look—as you are at this moment is who you are in life—weak, faltering, and fractured. He paused, watching her emotional pain. "You know I'm right . . ."

Tears welled, yet she refused to let them fall. He was enjoying every second of what he was saying, letting her know he still had control over her. She imagined he took more than a modicum of delight when she realized he was the mastermind of Brian's kidnapping. How painful it was. He knew she would beat herself up about not recognizing the clues right in front of her—to his way of thinking, she was too wrapped up with her psycho babble to look at a case from a black and white perspective.

"Time's up . . ." The guard lifted Rifkin by the arm, escorting him to the door.

The ex-sergeant latched onto the door jamb with his

fingers, then turned to Colbie. "You're a broken woman, Colbie Colleen—you just don't know it . . ."

****

Colbie sat in her car, knuckles white as she gripped the wheel, tears staining her cheeks. Even though she was in Rifkin's presence for only fifteen minutes, he managed to verbally eviscerate her, stripping her of all dignity—and, it was exactly what he meant to do.

She hoped it would have gone differently—more like the way Brian was dealing with Remington's being back in his life. But, as she scrutinized the difference on that hot summer day in her car, she realized meeting with Rifkin was a mistake only she could make. No matter how she tried to convince herself otherwise, her sole reason for visiting him in prison was to free herself. *God! I rehearsed it so many times! How could I have thought he might be glad to see me? Am I really weak? Am I really broken?*

Even she didn't know the answers to her questions, and Colbie realized then she was at a crossroads—ever since her private world shattered when she learned Sarge wasn't who she thought, she was wracked with self-doubt, unable to shake feelings of rejection. Of course, she did her best to hide it, and no one knew she was an emotional wreck at times—even Brian. She got so good at hiding her feelings, unworthiness became the norm. It was like living her childhood all over again—and, as she sat there contemplating how everything could have turned so wrong, she stepped effortlessly into her shadow world. A world where she was safe, and emotions weren't toxic and debilitating. A world where she felt loved, deserving, and safe as she identified with her past.

It had been a long time.

****

Growing up, Nicole Remington thought she had everything. After all, she didn't want for a thing, and the world was at her fingertips thanks to being born with a silver spoon. As a youngster, she didn't really know she was privileged, but she knew she could ask her parents for anything, and she would get it. It wasn't until she was in junior high she realized money meant power, and it was a realization that rocked her world. It was then she understood the true meaning of her last name—Champagne. It smacked of money, and Nicole embraced it like an old friend.

As she progressed through high school, she was known for fashionable clothes and expensive cars. Every year she had a new European model sitting in the Champagne driveway, and only those in her inner circle were graced with an occasional ride. But, she didn't gain a grip on her wealth until she attended a prestigious ivy league school on the East Coast—it was there she learned to use it to her best advantage.

It was there she met—then married—Harold Remington.

Although she didn't know it then, her husband would become a mainstay in her father's banking business—but, only after the old man died. As soon as Reggie learned Harold was in the market to try out his new college skills, he wasted no time bringing him on board. "We'll rise to the top together," he claimed, as they toasted with champagne on his first day on the job.

Rise, they did.

Within a few years, Nicole and Harold Remington were sought after for interviews at charity events and, quite often, the toast of the town. Society columns chattered endlessly about what she wore as well as the size of their charity donations—until the randy Harold was caught with his pants down.

They chattered about that, too.

Nicole always suspected, but chose to ignore her husband's roving eye. As long as he was on her arm for important events, the truth was she could care less about what he was doing in his free time. Unfortunately, only a few years after tying the knot, Nicole realized she made a dreadful mistake—Harold wasn't the man she thought he was, and there was a nefarious side to his personality she didn't find intriguing. She didn't find his pathological lying intriguing, either, and, before they reached their fifth anniversary, they were sleeping in separate bedrooms. Yes, she tried to talk to her brother about it, but he was too blinded by the amount of money Harold managed to bring into the bank—clients always on the QT, never named in yearly financial reports, or otherwise.

By their tenth anniversary, it was a foregone conclusion the marriage was over. As both anticipated, theirs was a messy, unpleasant divorce, Nicole recognizing a side of her husband she didn't know existed. His level of manipulation was masterful, and he didn't take it well when she tipped him off she was onto his game. A few threats later, he spent a couple of nights in the county jail for slapping her around, and he wondered how she dared bring their lives to the society pages.

So, after all was said and done, Nicole opted to keep her married name mainly because that's how everyone knew her. When she decided to jump into the world of real estate, wealthy connections played well for her and, before she knew it, she achieved number one in top sales circles. Harold, however, chose to split the country altogether, heading for the Alps as soon as the ink was dry on the divorce decree. "There's nothing for me here," he joked as he packed his last suitcase. "If I need anything, I'll call you . . ."

And, that was that.

But, there was one thing that took Nicole by surprise—she missed being married. She missed conversations about who was rising to the top in their social circles, as well as people making names for themselves by sponsoring and funding charity events. She missed arriving for tennis with a man on her arm—and, most of all, she missed the occasional moments by the fire when things were good. When she felt safe—and, warm.

It was when she met Al Vincent things started to change.

Vincent was a man who knew what he wanted, so when Nicole called his company, Optimum Security, to secure Reginald's home for a charity event, he was more than happy to comply. As soon as he hung up, he Googled her name, thrilled to find out she was in real estate—she would be perfect for what he had in mind.

He was right.

Theirs was a whirlwind romance—Nicole bought a unit in a brownstone Vincent owned, thinking she would get to see more of him since they were living in the same building. Both were busy with their own careers, but Vincent was so charming when they did get together, she couldn't help but melt every time she was in his arms.

He was a man every woman wanted.

****

"You look a little pale—you feeling okay?" Brian took a hard look at Colbie as she placed her purse and keys on the library table by the door.

"Just a little headache, that's all . . ." She couldn't look at him.

"How about if I draw you a bath—that always works!"

Before she could say no, he jumped up and headed for the bathroom and, within moments, she heard the rush of water.

Maybe a hot bath is just what I need, she thought as she kicked off her shoes. Her meeting with Rifkin took a toll on her and, by the time she wrapped up the investigation for the day, she could feel herself plunge deeper into despair.

"You're good to go in five minutes," Brian reported, wiping his hands on a towel. Again, he looked at her—something was off.

"Thanks—you're right. A bath sounds perfect!" She planted a peck on his cheek. "I think I'll lie down afterwards—okay with you?"

"Okay? Of course, it's okay—can I get you anything?"

She smiled, and headed for the bathroom. "Not a thing—I think I just need to close my eyes . . ."

The water was still hot by the time she crawled into the claw-foot tub and, as soon as she submerged her shoulders, she felt the tension begin to recede. Colbie closed her eyes, allowing the water's warmth to heal her body and mind. *How could he have been so cruel? Does he hate me that much?* Her thoughts tumbled, each one surfacing a new hurt. She couldn't remember feeling so exposed since her high school years, and she tried to fight the dark place her thoughts wanted her to go.

A fight she might not win.

****

There's a lot to be said for a bath and a good night's sleep—the following morning, Colbie awakened refreshed, ready to tackle the day. She and Brian agreed they'd start their days together to keep their relationship on track, but it was also a great way to plan everything they had to do. *God! What I'd give to have Tammy here*, she thought as she spread papers on the kitchen table.

"Okay—who did you research yesterday?" She reached for the cream.

"It was background research mostly . . ."

"Anything interesting?"

"Not really—except for Nicole Remington's husband." Brian waited for her reaction.

"Husband? What about him? I knew she was married, but I don't know much—what did you find out?"

"Well, Harold Remington is an interesting guy—how much do you know? No sense in repeating something you already have stashed in your brain . . ." He grinned, and poured himself a second cup of coffee.

"I know they married, and were part of the upper crust. Then, they divorced ten years later—that's about it . . ."

Brian scrolled the document on his laptop down a few pages. "Cool—let's pick it up here . . ." He squinted at the screen, moving the cursor to just the right spot.

Colbie watched, as he tried to focus. "You need glasses, you know . . ."

He sat back, eyeing her intently. "I . . ."

"Don't even try to argue the point! I'll make an appointment for you tomorrow . . ." She watched as a small grin formed. "You know I'm right . . ."

"Okay! Okay! You win!" He couldn't help laughing. Besides, she was willing to make the appointment for him, so the least he could do was go. He was pleased to see her back to her old self—he didn't tell her, but the previous evening? He was concerned. She wasn't the same Colbie who left that morning, and he had no doubt something happened—what changed, he didn't have a clue.

She looked at him fondly from across the table. "Back to work—what else did you find out about Harold Remington?"

"The first thing I found interesting was when he and Nicole decided to split the sheets, the first place he headed was the Alps . . ."

Colbie's eyebrows shot up as she realized the possible significance. "As in the 'Swiss' Alps?"

"The same . . ."

They were silent for a moment, thinking about connections. Was it a coincidence? Colbie tended to think it was not.

"Why did they get divorced in the first place?"

"The usual—irreconcilable differences. At least, that's what it was at first blush . . ."

"What was it at second blush?"

Brian paused, making sure he was getting his facts right. He squinted at the screen momentarily, then refocused on Colbie. "It seems Harold had interesting friends—friends Nicole couldn't stand . . ."

"Why didn't she like them?"

"Because they were from what she considered the other side of the tracks. She knew for a fact Harold was involved in drugs, but she couldn't prove it."

"Did she try to prove it?"

"Yep—I pulled court documents, and she made no bones about the fact her husband was deeply steeped in the drug trade . . ."

Colbie sat back, and sipped her coffee. "Sounds like sour grapes to me . . ."

Brian nodded. "That what I thought, until two thugs from a motorcycle gang showed up, threatening her within an inch of her life."

"As in a Hell's Angel's kind of gang?" Instantly, the image of a motorcycle in Brian's vision sprang to the forefront of her mind.

"Apparently, they scared her so bad, she didn't report it until she brought it up in the divorce proceedings."

"Too bad—if that's the truth, she should have reported it right away . . ."

Brian smiled. "Is that the ex-cop in you talking?"

"Maybe—but, you have to admit, it makes sense. Was she fabricating something she knew would have an impact on the court, or did it really happen?"

"You tell me—what do you think?"

Colbie thought for several moments before answering. "I think it happened—remember your vision of a motorcycle, and a pool of blood?"

"Holy crap! I forgot about that!"

She nodded. "See what I mean? I wasn't sure about what you were seeing in your vision, but now I don't have any doubt . . ."

"Yeah—but what does it mean?"

"Good question. I don't know, but I can tell you this— the motorcycle has something to do with Harold Remington. Now it's up to us to find out . . ."

CHAPTER SIX

C olbie couldn't get Brian's vision of the motorcycle out of her mind as she rolled through interview after interview with witnesses, as well as cops who were on the case. If it weren't for her professional reputation as one of the best psychological profilers in the business, getting anyone to talk within the police department would have been a challenge. But, as luck would have it, Colbie knew one of the sergeants at the precinct, and he paved the way. Still, even with all the new information, the motorcycle was stuck in her mind, and it wasn't going anywhere.

Ten days passed since Harold Remington piqued their interest. Summer got hotter, and residents looked forward to cooling rain, if that were possible. Colbie enjoyed the times she and Brian ate meals in restaurants—at least they were air conditioned. As perfect as their little craftsman home was, it was hot—uncomfortably hot.

Colbie and Brian agreed it was her job to figure out why Harold Remington took off for the Swiss Alps after his divorce before anybody could spit. But, she had to be careful—Nicole Remington wasn't stupid, and it wouldn't take her long to figure out Colbie was keeping something from her. Remington made it clear she wanted to be kept apprised about every facet of the investigation, and Colbie couldn't blame her—after all, her services were costing Remington a pretty penny. It was reasonable to require a line-item accounting of every dollar—even so, there were things Colbie had to keep to herself, and interest in Harold Remington was one of them.

Brian learned through his research Harold continued to play a part in the Champagne banking interests. And, playing a part was exactly what it appeared to be—Remington clearly enjoyed the jet-setter life, sparing no expense when it came to toys and women. *Perhaps they're the same thing,* Colbie thought as she opened the car door. Her ten-thirty appointment was in thirty minutes and, even if traffic were light, she knew she couldn't get there on time. Just as she was about to dial the number of her contact, her cell buzzed.

Tammy!

"Hey, you! What took you so long to call?" Colbie was thrilled to hear from her, but hearing Tammy's voice made her instantly aware just how much she relied on her ex-assistant when she was working a case.

"You know—unpacking."

Colbie's radar pinged. "Are you okay?"

Silence.

"Tammy? Are you okay? If something's wrong, you can tell me . . ." Colbie thought she heard a muffled sob—

something was definitely wrong.

She tried again, her voice softer. "Tammy? You can't fool me—I know something's wrong. Just tell me . . ."

Another sob. "Gary left me . . ."

"Left you? You've only been there a few months!"

"I know . . ."

"Tammy—what happened?" But, as she spoke, she already knew. "He cheated on you?"

The voice on the other end hesitated. "The second week we were here!"

The anguish in Tammy's voice was more than Colbie could bear. "Are you still in Florida?"

"Yes . . ."

Colbie paused, wondering if she should ask the question. "Will you come here? I'll pay for the move—I really need you right now, and I think you need me . . ."

Tammy said nothing for nearly a minute. "I don't know, Colbie . . ."

"What's not to know? We can be working together by the end of the week—what do you say?"

"What about Chase?"

"What about him?"

"He goes back to school in the fall . . ."

"Stop making excuses not to come—we'll get him in the best school. I promise . . ."

That was all Tammy needed to hear. "Oh, Colbie—you're saving my butt again! I don't know what to say . . ."

"There's nothing to say—how about if I give you my credit card number? You know the drill—make the reservation, and let me know when you're going to arrive." Colbie paused. "And, use that same card to make living arrangements—if you need Brian or me to check anything out for you, just let us know . . ."

Sobbing, Tammy agreed, promising to be back with Colbie by the end of the week.

Excellent! Colbie thought as she pushed the ignition. *Together again . . .*

****

Rumor had it they were in for a cool, rainy spell. It was about time, too—even people who were normally cheery couldn't wait for a solid week of clouds and rain. Colbie just wished it waited until she got Tammy settled in a cute bungalow with a fabulous view of the water. True, it was on the expensive side, and Tammy resisted—but, Colbie insisted. It was the least she could do to have the most important member of her team back in the saddle.

"Are you settled?" Colbie sat back in her office chair, looking at her newly-relocated assistant.

"Barely—and, thanks for setting up a nanny for Chase—

he really likes her . . ."

"That's important—she seemed great when Brian and I interviewed her . . ." Colbie eyed the young woman who looked as if she'd aged ten years in the last few months. Stress tugged at the corners of her lips, and her usually upbeat personality seemed to succumb to defeat.

Work, Colbie figured, was the only antidote.

****

She knew they would have to fly to Switzerland sooner or later—she just hadn't counted on its being sooner.

"I think we should leave at the beginning of the week—what do you think?" Colbie didn't look up as she checked out flights on her laptop. "I think we can be ready by then, don't you?"

Brian glanced at her, and grinned. "Whatever you say—Tammy can take care of things here, so I don't see any reason why not . . ."

"Perfect . . ." She took off her glasses, and looked at him. "I can't believe our luck—having Tammy here, I mean. That tells me we're on the right track . . ."

"What do you mean?"

"Can't you feel it? Ever since we dug deeper into Harold Remington, I just know we're on the right trail . . ."

Brian ran his fingers through his hair, then readjusted his ball cap. "I have to agree with you there—I'm not saying things are crystal clear, but I agree. The fact he took off for the Alps as soon as the divorce went through is suspicious enough . . ."

Colbie nodded. "It's going to be tricky, though—I'm not sure how we're going to get the information we need. I can't imagine the higher-ups in the banking industry will have loose lips . . ."

"I thought of that, too—can Nicole put you on to any contacts?"

"She already did—I have a list. In fact. I'll get in touch with them this afternoon, if possible . . ."

"What do you know about them?"

"Not much . . ." Colbie fished through her files, then flipped through the steno pad on her desk. "Ah—here they are . . . the first guy on Nicole's list is Christoph Anderegg, so I'll start with him . . ."

"What's his story?"

"He's on the board of Reginald Champagne's RNG Bank of Zurich and, from what I understand, he's been a friend of the family for years."

"Being a friend for years, unfortunately, doesn't guarantee a damned thing . . ." Brian looked expectantly at Colbie. "Any feelings? Do you think he's on our side?"

She thought for a moment, tapping into her intuitive mind. "I don't pick up anything negative about him—I think he's a good source of information for us . . ."

"Well, that's a start—let me know if you get in touch with him. I'm off to do a little research of my own . . ." With that, Brian was up, heading for the door.

"What kind of research?"

He grinned, leaving her wondering.

****

Neither Colbie nor Brian looked forward to the flight to Zurich. If they were lucky, they could make it in about twelve and a half hours—which stretched Brian's patience by about nine hours. Colbie? She was marginally better, counting on sleeping for at least half the travel time—besides, she knew once they landed, sleep would be elusive as they embroiled themselves in the case.

Taking the earliest flight possible put them on the ground in the middle of the night Zurich time and, by the time they arrived at their hotel, they'd been up for nearly twenty-four hours. Both agreed to hit the sack before unpacking, hoping to catch several hours of shuteye in an effort to combat jet lag. "It doesn't make any difference how brilliant we are," Colbie mentioned to Brian on the plane. "If we're tired, brilliance flies out the window . . ."

But, catching a few winks was easier said than done. The moment Colbie hit the sack, her mind brimmed with images she didn't understand. Eyes closed, her legs twitched as symbols appeared then receded, never allowing enough time to figure out their meanings. But, of one thing she was certain—they weren't good. Each appeared dark and foreboding, making her second-guess her decision to take the case as she tried in vain to clear her mind.

Finally surfacing to reality, her heart raced as she tried to make sense of the flickering visions—they were unlike anything she previously experienced. She glanced at Brian lying next to her, his breathing measured, already in a deep sleep. After fleeting disappointment, she realized how she looked forward to discussing her visions with him—up until their current case, Brian never exhibited interest in learning what she could do. Yes, he learned to believe in it—but, try it himself? She never thought she'd see the day.

Colbie lay quietly, suddenly thinking about Harold Remington. Her gut told her he was the foundation of their case, but she also had the feeling he was going to be difficult to access. Before leaving Seattle, she had a subtle conversation with Nicole, trying to glean as much info as possible about her ex-husband. But, what surprised Colbie was Nicole's reticence to discuss it. *Is she still in love with him*, she wondered, *or does she still care?* Either way, the result was the same—chasing Harold Remington would be like chasing a fading apparition.

Unless, of course, she set up the perfect scenario.

****

"I don't give a rat's ass! Get it done!"

Harold Remington's face turned an indescribable shade of persimmon as he eyed his two best men. He didn't care how much it cost, he wanted results, and he wanted them within the next twenty-four hours—or, sooner. "They're on the ground . . ."

Twice he repeated the information from his source to make certain there weren't any screw-ups. However, in spite of his warnings to return with satisfactory results, Harold knew he could trust them. Twenty years in his employ, and they hadn't disappointed him yet—still, he didn't want there to be a first time.

"Twenty-four hours isn't much time to acquire intel," the elder investigator reminded him. "You know we'll get much more if we take our time—we know they're going to be here a while, so why not hang back?"

The second investigator nodded. "Makes sense to me," he advised, glancing at his boss.

Remington wasn't used to their suggesting something opposing his plan or strategy—and, he wasn't sure he liked it. But, they would succeed, no matter what, so perhaps it was time to acquiesce. "Alright—you have until the end of the week." He paused, leveling a serious stare at each of the two men. "I want to know everything—tail their every move, even if it means you have to go 'round the clock . . ."

Without further conversation, Remington handed each man a folder, complete with dossiers and pictures, before showing them the door with a sweep of his hand. By extending his time line, he knew he created a time bomb, and he wasn't the least bit comfortable with the few extra days.

Both investigators nodded. "You got it . . ."

****

"At least I'm not as tired as I thought I would be . . ." Colbie reached for the cream, then sweetener as she stirred her coffee with the handle of her fork—she didn't have a spoon.

"Could've fooled me—you never take cream in your coffee . . ."

She smiled as she stirred absentmindedly, thinking of what they needed to accomplish that day. "Well, considering I got only four hours of sleep, I think I'm entitled . . ."

"Agreed—so, what's up? Should we split up, or stay together?"

"I was just thinking about that—let's stick together for today, then go our separate ways tomorrow . . ."

Brian eyed her. "Fine with me—why do you think that's best?" He watched carefully as she struggled momentarily for an answer. Ever since she arrived home with that horrific headache weeks earlier, there was something different about her. She wasn't the same. In fact, on some days, she retreated to their bedroom under the auspices of needing a quiet place to think—but Brian couldn't help thinking there was more to it. Over the last weeks, he noticed she asked his opinion on every little thing as if she weren't sure if she'd make the right decision. Even as he sat across from her, there was a slight sag to her shoulders—a defeat he hadn't seen before.

"It's mostly a safety thing—something's been bugging me since we got here, but, no matter how hard I try, I can't pick up on it . . ." Colbie paused, thinking of how to broach her dark visions. "Last night—this morning—as soon as my head touched the pillow, I was on sensory overload . . ."

"So—why's that any different than any other night?" He meant his question as a joke, but her scathing look told him she perceived it otherwise.

"The visions were dark—frightening, really—and I have the distinct impression we're about to discover something truly evil . . ."

From the look on her face, Brian knew she was serious. "Evil? As in . . ."

"That's just it—I don't know. I couldn't make sense of any of the impressions I received last night. All I know is we need to watch our backs . . ."

Brian sighed slightly. He didn't like the sound of anything evil, and it occurred to him he hadn't considered the possible negative side of Colbie's visions. Of course, he knew she had to protect herself, but, if the symbols she talked about were truly evil, then her protection wasn't working. "If that's the case, he commented, "then I don't think it's a good idea for us to separate at any time we're here . . ."

Colbie nodded. "You may be right—but, we'll get more done if we split up. I know how to take care of myself . . ."

"That may be, but I still don't like it. Can you remember anything of your visions? Maybe if you describe them to me, I can throw in my two cents . . ."

Colbie closed her eyes as she fidgeted in her chair trying to recall what permeated her mind only a few hours earlier. "A cemetery—but I don't have any idea of where it is . . ."

"Can you read a name on the headstone?"

"No—it's very small, as if it's a family plot of some sort."

"Is it around here—close to the city?"

She remained silent for a few moments before answering. "It's not far—and, I can hear church bells . . ."

It didn't take Brian long to figure out what she was seeing. "It seems like a small, church cemetery to me . . ."

Colbie nodded. "I think you're right," she commented as she opened her eyes. "But, if that's the case, it's going to be a needle in a haystack gig . . ."

"Maybe—but, we can't let that stop us." Brian again watched her carefully. Would she accept the difficulty of what they had before them, ready to fight? Or, would she back down, and find another way?

"What I do know, however, is the cemetery feels weird—not like a regular cemetery . . ."

CHAPTER SEVEN

66 Christoph Anderegg, please . . ." Colbie stood in front
of the receptionist's massive curved desk, taking note
of everything in the room as well as the middle-aged
woman looking at her expectantly.

"Do you have an appointment?" The receptionist's
English was surprisingly good with only the slightest hint
of an accent.

Colbie nodded. "Yes—at 10:30."

"Please have a seat—his assistant will be with you
shortly." She picked up the phone, and tapped three numbers
as Colbie chose a chair nearest flawless glass doors leading
to upper level executive offices. *The Champagnes have good
taste*, she thought as her fingers brushed the expensive
upholstery. There was no doubt whose decorating taste ruled

supreme when the building was last remodeled—gone were essences of the past, modern-traditional taking its place. Colbie instantly recognized similarities to the Champagne mansion stateside—tasteful, with just the right amount of class.

"Colbie Colleen?"

"Yes . . ."

"Please come with me . . ." Colbie obeyed, following the young woman through the glass doors into a hallway lined with oil-on-canvas portraits of RNG Bank of Zurich executives. Expensive carpet ran the length of the corridor, perfectly placed so the exquisite marble floor made an impression, but didn't show off.

Moments later, the young woman stopped at another set of glass doors—clearly, the inner sanctum. As they entered, the buzz of business as usual diminished, offering a slightly eerie reverence until a huge man with a booming voice greeted her. "Ms. Colleen?" He offered his hand. "Christoph Anderegg . . ."

Colbie nodded and accepted the handshake, her hand nearly disappearing in his. "Thank you for taking the time to meet with me—I apologize for the short notice . . ." She smiled her warmest smile as he showed her into his office, his secretary quietly closing the door behind them.

"Nonsense—the truth is I was expecting your call. Nicole clued me in, allowing me time to rearrange my schedule." Christoph motioned to a chair. "Please—make yourself comfortable . . ."

After a moment or two to get situated, Colbie decided the best approach was to dive right in. "Did Nicole tell you why I needed to touch base with you?"

"She did—and, I'll do everything I can to bring Reginald's killer to justice . . ."

"I appreciate that—I'm afraid, however, I don't have much to go on, so far, and I'm counting on you to fill me in—not only about Reginald, but your thoughts about who decided murder was the way to go . . ."

"I don't mind telling you," Anderegg warned, "I'll get the son of a bitch who did this . . ."

Colbie eyed the hulking man behind the desk. As she shook his hand, she didn't feel he was something other than what you see is what you get. "Well, I'm confident my partner and I will make headway, but our progress will be dependent on connecting with the right people. I'm hoping, Mr. Anderegg, you will pave the way for me . . ."

"I'll do what I can, of course—did Nicole give you names?"

"She did . . ." Colbie reached into her purse, pulling out a small piece of paper with several names carefully handprinted. She slid the paper across the desk, paying particular attention to Anderegg's reaction as he read it.

"I know everyone on this list—some better than others, but I don't think any of them will deny my request to speak to you." In fact, Christoph Anderegg knew that for certain—denying his request was clearly a bad idea.

"Perfect—now, how about if we switch gears? Who do you think is responsible for Reginald's murder?"

Anderegg sat quietly aligning his thoughts for Colbie's benefit, eyes cast downward toward his desk. Finally, he looked up. "Even though Reginald was one hell of a guy, he had enemies." He paused, weighing the possible consequences of his next statement. "Inside and out . . ."

Colbie tried not to register surprise at his candor. "You mean inside and outside of your banking organization?"

His eyes locked onto hers. "That's exactly what I mean. Of course, all I can do is point you in what I believe to be the right direction . . ."

Colbie refused to break his gaze. "I understand—it's up to us to ferret it out . . ."

"Indeed, it is . . ." Suddenly, Anderegg rose, and showed Colbie to the door. "Remember these numbers," he whispered. "Four, seven, eight . . ."

Colbie turned to him before she was all the way out the door. "Their significance?"

"Think of our conversation today as you continue your investigation—that's all I can say . . ."

With that, Anderegg transferred Colbie to his assistant. "Good luck," he said with a smile. "If there's anything I can do . . ."

That was it.

Nothing about Reginald, Remington, or anyone else Colbie planned to interview.

Anderegg's assistant accompanied Colbie to the massive front doors, and moments later Colbie stood on a street bathed in sunshine, rehashing the quickest meeting of her career. *Christoph Anderegg is an intelligent man*, she thought as she hailed a cab. *And, I know as sure as I'm standing here, there's something he's not telling me . . .*

****

She hardly had time to change her clothes when Brian blew through the door. Even though they discussed sticking together, doing so didn't fit into their timeframe—besides, Colbie didn't need babysitting, and she was pretty sure Brian didn't, either.

"Lucy—I'm home!"

Colbie could hear the smile in his voice, and she couldn't help grinning herself. "How did it go?" She watched as he threw his jacket on a chair, then plopped beside her on the couch.

"Good—but, I didn't get much. I don't think Bruder knows anything . . ." He handed her the man's dossier.

"Really?" She flipped through the pages. Bruder was second on the list Nicole gave her—the same list she showed to Anderegg—and she had a hard time believing he didn't know anything. "Tell me everything—what's he like?"

"Small—he reminds me of a skittish mouse scurrying from corner to corner. He had a hard time sitting still, and his fingers were constantly fiddling with the corner of a stack of papers on his desk . . ."

"Nerves?"

"Maybe—but I have a feeling he's that way all the time."

"A feeling, huh?" She smiled, unable to resist the dig. "What's his position at the bank?"

"Managing Director of Investment Banking—a big gun

for such an unassuming man . . ."

"What did he have to say about Reginald Champagne?"

Brian took a moment to recall his time with Bruder. "He said he didn't know Reginald well—according to him, he joined the company only a couple of years ago, and he rarely had the opportunity to see Reggie, let alone spend time with him."

Colbie arched a brow. "That doesn't make sense—as head of investment banking? I'd think he and Reginald would be joined at the hip . . ."

Brian looked sideways at her as he scrunched lower into the couch cushions. "Not sure I follow you . . ."

"Think about it—banks are nothing but investments. Anyone who has as much clout as Bruder would certainly be in touch regularly with the bank's top execs . . ." She thought for a minute. "And—it seems to me—his behavior doesn't indicate a bank executive exuding confidence. Maybe he has something to hide . . ."

"Well—you're right about that. When I asked him for his opinion about what happened to Champagne, all he said was it was a shame it happened . . ."

"That's it?"

"Yep—I told you I didn't get much. What about you—how was your meeting with Anderegg?"

Colbie tucked a pillow under her arm. "It was interesting—but he left me with more of a puzzle, than anything . . ."

"A puzzle?"

Colbie nodded. "Not to mention it was the shortest

meeting I ever had—I was in and out within five minutes . . ."

"So—what did he say in those five minutes?"

"Well, he told me he would do anything he could to bring Champagne's killer to justice, and he wants to catch the son of a bitch who offed him . . ."

"What's so puzzling about that?"

"Nothing—but then he said Reginald had enemies inside and outside the banking industry."

"He suspects someone from the inside?"

"Yep—but I get the feeling inside leads to the outside. When I gave him the list of people Nicole told us to talk to, he admitted he knew everyone on it, some better than others. But, the names on that list weren't just banking related . . ."

"Weird—so, that's the puzzle?"

"That's part of it—it was pretty obvious Anderegg didn't want to say, suggest, or admit anything concrete. But, here's what's really strange—as I was leaving, he whispered in my ear, advising me to remember the numbers four, seven, and eight . . ."

Brian repeated the numbers out loud. "Do you know what he was talking about?"

Colbie shook her head. "Nope—not a clue . . ."

****

By the end of the week, sunshine turned to rain, putting a damper on Colbie's and Brian's onsite investigations. Colbie took advantage of staying indoors by updating Nicole on their progress, although she didn't have much to report. "Did you talk to any of the names on the list," Nicole asked, eager to hear what she had to say. Colbie confirmed she did, and she was looking forward to speaking with Harold Remington.

"He might be difficult to get ahold of," Nicole casually commented. "If he's anything like he was before, he'll be partying at God knows where . . ."

"Still—I need to talk to him the same as the other people on the list. So, if you get wind of where he is, please let me know immediately . . ."

"Why would I get wind of where he is?"

Colbie sensed Nicole's bristling—*why such a strong reaction*, she wondered as she listened to her client. "You never know, Nicole—he might call you out of the blue. Either way, I'm sure I'll track him down . . ."

"Do you think he's involved in Reginald's murder?"

Colbie's radar pinged. "I don't have any idea—right now I'm treating him just the same as anyone on the list . . ."

After a few more questions for her client, Colbie rang off, her intuitive senses on high alert.

Something wasn't right.

****

Harold Remington listened to the voice on the other end, knuckles clenched as he gripped his cell. "What do you mean there was only one? Two were on Swiss soil four hours ago—who's missing?"

His seasoned investigator held the phone away from his ear while Remington ranted. "We never got eyes on both targets," he admitted. "Only Fischer, and we tailed him to a small town outside of Zurich . . ."

"Town? What town?"

"Gruyères . . ."

"Then what? Where did he go?"

The investigator hesitated, knowing his boss wasn't going to like what he had to say. "We lost him . . ."

He was right.

Harold Remington seethed as he processed the information. "How the hell could you lose one, stinkin' guy?"

"The streets were crowded and, by the time we parked and caught up with him, he was gone . . ."

"Didn't one of you get out to keep an eye on him while the other parked?" No response. Remington couldn't believe what he was hearing! Everything depended on his two targets being together and, if his men couldn't locate the one who strangely went missing, all bets were off.

He would have to wait.

CHAPTER EIGHT

Gruyères was stunning at that time of year. Streets bustled with tourists as well as locals, and trees were beginning to show signs of preparing for a long, expected winter.

Colbie and Brian tipped their faces to the last warm rays of the sun as they enjoyed cups of Swiss hot chocolate at a street-side café—even though they were in the throes of their investigation, it felt good to take time to relax a little.

"Let's walk," Colbie suggested as she drained the last of the best hot chocolate she could imagine.

Brian nodded. "Good idea—I need to get some exercise! I think I just put on a few extra pounds . . ."

"Me, too," Colbie laughed. "That stuff was rich!"

Within thirty minutes, they lingered at a crossroad—although they weren't far from the main streets, the countryside gently appeared, quaint buildings of the town behind them. A stone church stood humbly on the diagonal corner, its turrets and red door gleaming in the late afternoon sun.

Brian looked at the scene across the road. "What a great pic! Do you have the good camera with you?" In awe of the bucolic scene, he wanted nothing more than to capture it on film.

"Yep!" Colbie reached into her bag, then dramatically presented the camera. "You don't think I would go anywhere without it, do you?"

"Not really . . ." He grinned, adjusted the camera to the light, and snapped several pictures from varying angles. As he walked across the road, he noticed something on the far side of the church. "Hey! Get a load of this!" He handed the camera to Colbie so she could zoom in. "Do you see what I see?"

"No—what are you looking at?"

"The cemetery! You can barely see it on the other side of the building . . ."

She focused the camera to the far side of the church. "You're right! Let's get over there—I want to see if it has something to do with my vision . . ."

"My thought, precisely . . ." Brian grabbed her hand, heading toward the heavy front doors of the chapel. "We should ask, however, before we start snooping around . . ." He tried to open the door, but it was locked.

"I thought the only church in town was the Saint-Pierre-aux-Liens—this one's much smaller, and it looks like it's more for the community. Not tourism . . ." Colbie stood on the church's walkway, drinking in everything she wanted to remember.

"Let's check out the cemetery . . ." Brian glanced at Colbie, surreptitiously monitoring her response. "I don't think anyone will mind . . ."

"Fine with me—if we get caught, you can talk your way out of it!"

As they rounded the far corner of the church, a weather-worn cemetery stood before them. Aged headstones revealed centuries of the dead, many leaning or toppling due to shifts in the ground below. No care. No maintenance. No flowers.

Colbie gently let go of Brian's hand, kneeling beside one of the gravestones, touching its surface with the palm of her hand. Closing her eyes, she allowed images to flood her intuitive mind, trying to connect them to her first vision of a cemetery. "I don't know," she commented to Brian. "Something feels—weird . . ."

"Weird? What do you mean?"

"I'm seeing the Scales of Justice . . ."

Brian thought for a moment. "Here? In Switzerland? Does that make sense?"

"I don't think location has anything to do with it . . ." She still knelt by the headstone, eyes closed. "There's something here that smacks of a lie—something isn't what it seems . . ."

"Is it ever?"

"Are you picking up on anything?" Since Brian's foray into her world, she knew he may see something valid. Something worthwhile.

He glanced at Colbie as the damp grass saturated the knees of her jeans. Offering a hand, he coaxed her up. "Now that you mention it, I am feeling something—and, it seems like something isn't welcomed here." He paused, glancing at the headstones. "Maybe it's us . . ."

Colbie stared at him. "That's exactly how I feel! That's what I meant when I said something is weird!"

Both stood silently in front of a small plot of markers, wondering about the lives of those who lay beneath. As the autumn sun dipped behind the mountains, Colbie and Brian realized they happened onto something big.

Now, if they could just figure out what is was.

****

That evening, Colbie entered her shadow world.

After discovering the small church cemetery, she felt unbalanced and, if she were to be completely honest, something chipped away at her confidence. No longer did she completely trust her intuition, and she felt it necessary to corroborate her visions by asking Brian if he witnessed the same things. *What was it Rifkin said? I'm weak?* She thought about that for a moment as she felt herself drift further into the world providing a cloak of comfort.

Maybe I am . . .

****

"Who's third on the list?"

"Mueller—Eric Mueller. He doesn't work at the bank, but Nicole indicated he's an acquaintance of Harold's. From what she told me, he used to piss her off simply because of his lack of manners. 'Boorish', she called him."

"Boorish? That's a word you don't hear often . . ."

"True—according to her, he was one of Harold's wrong-side-of-the-tracks friends. Apparently, he hit on her more than once during the few times she was in Zurich, and Harold didn't seem to think anything of it—clearly, it was okay with him."

Brian's face registered his disgust. "Nice—so, who's going to tackle him? I'm game if you have something else to do . . ."

Colbie studied the names on the list. "Well—if you'll interview Mueller, that allows me time to interview and check off the next one . . ."

"Name?"

"Gaspar Fischer—although, he doesn't work at RNG Bank of Zurich . . ." She hesitated, thinking about a possible connection. "He works at one of the top vault companies . . ."

"What do you know about him, so far?"

"Not much—my interview with him will be a fishing expedition, that's for sure." Colbie thought for a minute. "In fact, Nicole told me Fischer travels a lot, so it may be tough to get ahold of him, at all . . ."

"Didn't Anderegg tell you he would make sure everyone on that list was cooperative?"

"Yes—although I confess it was more of a feeling I got. His importance in and out of the banking industry is impressive, and I get the distinct impression when he commands someone to jump, their response is, 'How high?'"

They spent the next hours planning and, by the time ten o'clock rolled around, Colbie and Brian were clear about what they had to accomplish the next day. Brian kissed her gently on the cheek and turned out his nightstand light while she lay in bed doubting her ability to get in touch with Gaspar Fischer. She didn't like having to receive permission from Anderegg—shouldn't she already have enough clout to convince him it would be in his best interest to grant her an interview?

Of course, she should.

****

So much for clout. Gaspar Fischer expressed no interest in speaking with her, ultimately putting her in front of Christoph Anderegg again. But, that was okay—the impromptu meeting provided the opportunity to discuss her interviews with those on the list, as well as to get his take on the validity of their information. Soon after her meeting with Anderegg, however, the next time she phoned Fischer for an interview, he stated a time and place.

In an hour.

****

It didn't give her much time. Slightly ill-prepared for the meeting, Colbie knew she was going to need to rely on her intuition, and she already had the feeling Fischer was a smooth operator—would he use those skills with her?

Probably.

From his picture in the dossier, she knew to look for a tall, lanky man—a string bean, really. He stood nearly six-five, and tipped in at no more than one sixty—and, as she studied his picture and information before the meeting, she had no doubt the beanpole vault executive would be on high alert. She already had an unpleasant feeling about him, although she had nothing to corroborate it, and she felt a darkness as she ran her hand over his picture. *What do you have to hide, Mr. Fischer?*

She knew there was something.

As she reached the front of the hole-in-the-wall tavern, she wondered why he didn't meet her in his office—it seemed the most likely place.

Putting her weight into the heavy door, she entered a dark, warm steak house, reminding her of her favorite restaurant stateside. It looked like crap on the inside, but even thinking about their ribeye steak medium rare made her mouth water.

"Good afternoon—how many?" A tall, blonde woman nodded in greeting, her hand poised gracefully on the hostess stand.

"Actually, I'm meeting someone—very tall . . ."

"Oh, yes—he's already here. Please—follow me . . ." The hostess snaked her way through empty tables and chairs to the back of the tavern. "Mr. Fischer? Your guest . . ."

Gaspar Fischer stood, politely dismissing the hostess with a nod. "Colbie Colleen, I presume?" He smiled, displaying a row of perfectly aligned teeth, slightly whiter than they should be. "Please, sit down . . ."

Colbie smiled warmly, thinking a brusque, professional approach may not be the best. "Thank you—I appreciate your seeing me on such short notice . . ."

Fischer studied her carefully as she made herself comfortable. "Unfortunately, I don't have much time, so perhaps we should order, then get down to business . . ."

Colbie agreed and, within minutes, the server left their table with two orders of the daily special. "Did you have an opportunity to speak with Christoph Anderegg?" She placed her napkin in her lap, directing her attention to Fischer.

"Briefly—he said you're looking into the death of Reginald Champagne . . ."

"That's correct—I have a list of names, and yours was fourth on that list. I'm hoping you can provide insight regarding his colleagues and friends, as well as what he might have been working on—was it something critical enough to get him murdered?"

Fischer smiled, although it dripped insincerity. "I know very little, Miss Colleen, about Reginald's personal life. As far as to what he was working on, I can only imagine . . ."

Listening to his patronizing voice, Colbie knew instantly she was getting nowhere. "Why do you think he was murdered," she interrupted. She held his gaze, noticing a slight glower flicker across his face. "Surely, you must have your own ideas . . ."

"Perhaps, but I know nothing concrete . . ."

"Then," she smiled, "I guess it's a good thing I'm not seeking anything concrete. What can you tell me about his banking associates? I know you're in the vault business, so I assume you worked closely with him . . ."

So much for the softer approach.

Gaspar Fischer's jaw set as the redheaded spitfire looked him directly in his eyes. There was something about her he didn't like, and it didn't take him long to figure out she was tenacious. She wasn't the least bit uncomfortable asking questions—questions he didn't feel like answering. "Indeed—we did work closely together, but that doesn't mean we were bosom buddies. We didn't socialize, and I rarely connected with him outside of our respective corporate positions."

"I see . . ." Colbie knew he was lying in his too-straight teeth. "Then, what can you tell me about Harold Remington? As I understand it, you're good friends . . ."

Fischer laughed. "Harold? Yes, indeed—we've known each other for years!" He paused as the server delivered their lunches, then struck off to greet new customers. "But, I'm afraid I don't understand—what does Harold have to do with Reginald's untimely demise?"

Colbie thought she detected a smarmy lilt in his voice as he asked his question. "I'm not sure—the fact he was married to Champagne's sister is reason enough to contact him, don't you agree?"

"I wouldn't know . . ." He checked his watch, subliminally letting her know she was on thin ice—ending their meeting would be the result if she continued with her line of questioning.

It was unfortunate for him his subtle intimidation did little to dissuade her. "I apologize if my questions seem abrupt—but, we only have an hour, and I need to learn as much as possible about Reginald as well as anyone else with whom he kept company—professional or personal."

Fischer patted his lips with his napkin. "I understand—but you're barking up the wrong tree. I know nothing. Our paths crossed with respect to business only, and unless you uncover something of magnitude, I suspect Reginald's passing will remain a mystery." He paused, then stood. "I'm afraid I must be going—but, please, finish your lunch. I already took care of the tab . . ." With that, he gracefully slipped into a black, calf-length wool coat, and departed after a slight bow to his guest.

"Just one more thing, if you don't mind . . ." It was a wild idea, but she gave it a shot anyway. "Have you ever been to Gruyères?"

"Gruyères? Of course—lovely place."

"I agree—I happened upon a beautiful, little church on the outside of town. Do you happen to know anything about it?"

"Church?" Fischer chuckled. "I'm afraid not—going to church isn't on my list of things to do." Again, he checked his watch. "I really must go—please excuse me . . ."

"Of course—thank you for your time . . ." Colbie watched him nod to the hostess as he strode through the door. *I don't trust that guy as far as I can throw him*, she thought, watching Fischer hail a cab. As he climbed in, he turned toward the large window of the tavern—even though she sat in the rear of the restaurant, she felt his eyes boring into her.

A warning.

CHAPTER NINE

Anyone who was anyone within the banking industry knew it was unwise to cross Harold Remington—Gaspar Fischer knew it, too. Still, with such worldly knowledge, money seemed to speak louder than underlying fear.

His relationship with Remington was exactly as he told Colbie Colleen—strictly business. What he didn't tell her was their contracts were outside the confines of banking regulations. *She doesn't know any more than when she walked in*, Fischer thought as he approached Remington's office. *Even so, I must tell him . . .*

He nodded to Remington's secretary, softly closing the door behind him.

"He's expecting you," she advised, without looking up.

Fischer studied her from head to toe, approving of what he saw. "You look particularly delicious today, Monique . . ."

"Thank you." Her voice was curt. Cold.

Fischer was just about to offer an evening of fine food to the young assistant as Remington's door opened. "Get your ass in here," he ordered before Fischer could get the invitation out of his mouth.

He nodded to the young woman. "Perhaps next time . . ."

"Leave her alone, Gaspar," Remington admonished as his assistant's cheeks flushed with embarrassment.

Fischer laughed. "You can't blame me for trying, can you?"

Remington stepped aside as Gaspar Fischer dramatically entered his office—the inner sanctum. Both men took their respective seats established years prior, Remington behind his desk, Fischer facing him. "So—what's so important?"

Fischer removed his gloves, laying them carefully on his lap. "What do you know about Colbie Colleen?"

"Who the hell is Colbie Colleen?"

"That's what I thought—so, you have no idea who she is, or what she does . . ."

"Get on with it Fischer—I don't need the drama . . ."

Fischer looked at his cuticles for a moment, then raised his eyes to meet Remington's. "Colbie Colleen is a highly regarded profiler and investigator . . ."

Remington didn't flinch.

"And," Fischer continued, "she's investigating the death

of Reginald Champagne . . ." He waited, knowing Remington would do one of two things—remain silent, digesting the information, or erupt in a raging tirade.

Luckily, he chose the former. "How do you know?"

"Because she called me several times to schedule an interview—something of which I had no intention of granting until Anderegg stuck his nose in . . ."

Harold Remington's eyes narrowed as he realized the situation. "What did you tell her?"

"Nothing—I said we were business partners, and we had no personal relationship, whatsoever . . ."

"Did she buy it?"

"I have no idea—and, I wasn't going to wait around to find out. I begged out of our meeting under the auspices of needing to catch a flight."

Harold Remington sat back in his cushy desk chair considering the possibilities. "Who turned her on to me?"

Fischer leveled a dramatic look at his colleague. "None other than Nicole . . ."

****

"So—what do you think? I can tell just by looking at you thoughts of Gaspar Fischer are swirling around in that pea brain of yours . . ."

Colbie laughed. "I'm that transparent?"

"Yep!" Brian studied his better half as she wrapped herself in a white, terrycloth bathrobe, admiring her ability to keep a sense of humor in serious situations. "You look tired . . ."

"I am—a little . . ." She slipped her feet into sheepskin slippers, then situated herself on the couch next to him. "So—what do I think? I think Gaspar Fischer is our first break . . ."

"Seriously? In what way?"

"Well—when I was reviewing his dossier, I ran my palm over his picture, and I was flooded with a dark feeling. Then, when I actually met him, I realized immediately he wasn't going to provide any information—the only thing I learned was he and Remington were business colleagues only."

"Do you think that's true?"

"Let's put it this way—I don't believe anything coming out of Fischer's mouth . . ."

Brian whistled softly. "Then you may be right—maybe Fischer is our first break . . ."

"I'd bet my last dollar on it—and, get this . . . as he was leaving our meeting, something told me to ask him about Gruyères."

"And?"

"I asked him if he knew of the little church with the cemetery . . ."

"What did he say?"

Colbie paused, recalling Fischer's attitude and words. "He said going to church wasn't his thing—but I know as sure as I'm sitting here, he's involved with that church one way or another . . ."

"That seems weird, though—how could a high-ranking executive like Fischer be involved in a church that barely holds fifty people? And, why?"

"I don't know—but, I'm sure as hell going to find out . . ."

****

What Fischer didn't know was he was a growing blip on Remington's radar. But, then again, why would he? There's a certain level of arrogance in many top-level officials or executives which, unfortunately, includes thinking they're impervious to all life can dish out.

Gaspar Fischer was one of them.

And, it was that arrogance Harold Remington counted on. He wasn't too pleased with Fischer's performance lately, and it was all he could do to not call him on it. But, doing so would be a fatal error—no, it was better to have his men tail him to determine exactly what he was up to. Remington supposed he should have felt some sort of—sadness—when he considered how his trust in Gaspar Fischer began to erode.

But, he didn't.

He really could have cared less—if a man can't prove his worth to his circle of confidants, then what good is he? Although Fischer's waning allegiance was obvious, no one within Remington's organization wanted to speak of such dishonesty. Distrust. Duplicity.

He thought for a moment before punching numbers on his phone.

What are you up to, Nicole?

****

"Tammy?" Colbie could barely hear her assistant as they struggled with a scratchy connection. "Have you heard anything from Nicole? I tried to reach her several times, but she's not returning my calls . . ."

"Really? That's weird—she called twice yesterday saying the same thing about you . . ."

Colbie hesitated, considering the challenges of an overseas call no matter how great the technology. "Did she leave a message?"

"No—but she sounded a little strange. I remember when I talked to her several years ago, she always commanded the conversation—not so much yesterday . . ."

"Did she sound upset?"

"In a way—but, more than that, she sounded . . . jittery. I could hear her voice quiver, but I didn't want to intrude by asking if anything were wrong . . ."

"Probably a good choice . . ."

"She left a number where she can be reached—she said she was going out of town for a couple of days." Tammy rattled off the number knowing full well Colbie didn't have a piece of paper. As much as her boss wanted Tammy to believe she changed her ways by using an actual tablet to take notes, Tammy pictured her digging in her purse for a gum wrapper to write on. "I'll text it to you—that way you'll have it at your fingertips . . ."

"Perfect—did she say where she was going?"

"Nope—and, I didn't ask."

If Colbie had to place a moniker on Nicole Remington, 'fearful' wouldn't be it. Still, no matter how much she tried to convince herself Nicole changed over the years, she couldn't quite bring herself to believe it. *Do people change? Drastically change?* One thing Colbie prided herself on was her ability to read true motives of her clients—but Nicole was different. *Maybe I'm losing my touch*, she thought as she listened to Tammy. It was a thought she had more than once over the last several weeks, and it made her feel uncomfortable in her own skin.

After another ten minutes of catching up on office tasks, Colbie hung up, her mind reeling. *What if Nicole's in on everything? What if she set me up?* It was a line of thinking not too far afield, and one Colbie hadn't previously considered for long. There was always the possibility, of course, but Colbie determined at the beginning of their investigation Nicole was a changed woman.

If that's not the case, how could I be so wrong?

****

Nicole Remington snatched her overnight bag from the trunk, scanning the cabin and its inky surroundings. Even though she called ahead to let the caretaker know of her arrival, ever since her last conversation with Harold, she couldn't trust anything in her life, and it was enough to make her head for the hills.

Soft lamplight illuminated the cabin's porch, it's log and stone construction reminding her of better times. Earlier times. As she climbed the steps, childhood memories flooded her thoughts, making her wonder how she could have found herself in such a situation. *Most likely to succeed, my ass*, she thought as the key turned easily in the lock. If her high school friends could see her now, they'd never believe it—especially Rebecca. Her nemesis since seventh grade, Rebecca Tomlinson would take great pleasure knowing of Nicole's recent past, never suspecting prison would have been in the cards for her—she'd thoroughly enjoy that tidbit of information. Always jealous of Nicole's material possessions, Rebecca tried more than once to insert herself into the prestigious group of girls, only to find herself shunned and disregarded.

Then came high school.

Things changed.

Rebecca changed her name to Becca, surrounding herself with friends harboring dark intentions. She stalked Nicole until Nicole's parents intervened, leaving her with a seething hatred she never ceased to display. And, although years passed, Nicole still remembered her wealth and social standing cocooning her like a safety net.

It was all she had.

The door opened easily, revealing life as she remembered it. When she was married to Harold, of course he wanted to update everything, and she had a fight on her hands when she refused. "It's the only thing left of my childhood," she told him, her voice an irritating whine. But, he didn't care— to him, the cabin smelled of age as well as a life he didn't know, and he was more than willing to let it go altogether. "Over my dead body," she murmured as memories sparked a tear or two as she stepped inside.

The caretaker and his wife prepared a lovely tray of cheese and fruit, a note stuck on the refrigerator to let her know. They also stocked deli turkey and roast beef, perfect for making a late-night sandwich—and, steaks were in the freezer, if Nicole felt so inclined. Employed by the Champagnes since the sixties, the aging couple still made every effort to make visitors feel at home, and they spared no effort when Nicole called to tell them she would be there for a few days.

She quickly hung up the few clothes she packed, then

stoked the fire which was down to its last embers. Stress began to drain from her body as she sat down with the elegant cheese tray, her conversation with Harold at the forefront of her mind. She couldn't help recalling Colbie's comment about the possibility of Harold's getting in touch with her, and she found it slightly off-putting the investigator was right.

The truth was she found the profiler rather insufferable, but she couldn't take that into consideration when finding the right person to take over her brother's murder investigation. Yet, all that aside, Colbie Colleen was the best in the business, and past differences were cast aside—she was just lucky Colbie accepted the case. If everything worked out according to plan, Nicole would learn who double-tapped Reginald as well as how to take Colbie down a few pegs for her involvement in bringing down the real estate scam.

Prison was something she would never forget, and she held Colbie Colleen directly responsible.

****

"Who's next on the list?" Brian refilled Colbie's coffee, then pushed the cream across the table.

"Before we get into that, let's go through who we talked to, so far . . ." Colbie flipped the pages of her tablet until she came to a page more scribbled on than the others. "Our first contact was Christoph Anderegg, and he's the one who told me to remember the numbers four, seven, and eight. He's a big gun, but I don't have a feeling he's involved in anything nefarious."

She thought for a minute before continuing. "The second person we—you—spoke to was Bruder. I don't remember his first name, but, according to you, he doesn't know anything."

"According to me?"

"Well—yes. I'm learning to trust your intuitive instincts, and if you say he's not involved, then that's good enough for me . . ."

Brian was stunned. Of all the things he thought he would never hear from Colbie's lips! "I'm honored . . ."

She grinned at him, then consulted the list again. "Third, you talked to Eric Mueller—I'm not so sure I'm ready to put him to rest yet—what do you think?"

"I'm with you—but, do I think he's the brains of some illicit operation? No—he's too much of a mouse . . ."

"From what you told me, that's what I think—but, he may be a person who is easily blackmailed. He may know more than we think without being an actual participant . . ."

Brian nodded. "Agreed—put him on the 'maybe' list." He watched as Colbie created another column on her paper. "Who's next?"

Colbie looked at him. "Number four—Gaspar Fischer."

Brian met her eyes, knowing in his gut Fischer was a main player. "As you said, he's our first real break—I think so, too. But, when it comes down to it, we have nothing to go on—all we have is feelings."

Colbie took several seconds before answering. "That's true, but I think if you surveil Fischer while I'm interviewing the next names on the list, we'll get the info we need . . ."

"Works for me—where do I start?"

"Good question—I know where his office is, although I haven't been there. And, I know he prefers to meet in out-of-the-way places such as the steakhouse. I get the distinct impression he tries to fly under the radar . . ."

"As if he has something to hide?"

"Exactly . . ."

Colbie and Brian gently held hands on the couch, each lost in thought. Without warning, Colbie heard Christoph Anderegg's voice in her intuitive mind. "Remember the numbers . . ."

Suddenly, she sat up, squeezing Brian's hand in excitement! "That's it! I'm positive—that's it!"

Brian snatched his hand away from her before she crushed a few fingers. "What's it?"

"The numbers! Anderegg's warning—at least it seemed like a warning. The numbers he told me to remember—four, seven, and eight! They correspond to the numbers on our list!"

Brian extended his hand. "Let me see . . ."

She handed him the legal pad, pointing excitedly to the numbered contacts. "Gaspar Fischer is number four!" She looked at Brian expectantly, waiting for his response.

"I think you're right," he murmured. "Let's see who's number seven and eight—maybe we should get right to them, and forget about the other numbers . . ."

Colbie nodded. "That's a good idea, but I'm not sure I'm ready to give up on the others. It only takes one nugget of information . . ."

Both sat silently, realizing they cracked the first clue in their case. Colbie rewound her two conversations with Christoph Anderegg, certain his calling attention to three numbers was their first break—and, it went hand-in-hand with Gaspar Fischer.

"You have the pad," Colbie finally stated. "Who're numbers seven and eight?"

Brian traced the numbers with his fingers. "Number seven is Jan Bachmann—eight is Gregor Hoffer . . ."

"I wasn't planning on skipping numbers—do we have dossiers on both men?"

Brian jumped up, heading for his messenger bag. "Yep— one for you and one for me," he commented, handing her a manila file folder. Yes, paper files were old-fashioned, but Colbie insisted on not counting on technology to tell her what she needed to know.

"Perfect . . ."

CHAPTER TEN

Three days at the cabin was just what she needed—time to think. Plan. Act. She decided before she arrived she wouldn't drink while there—not even a glass of chardonnay. No—her mind needed to be clear to decide her next move.

Around four o'clock on her last day, Nicole wandered down the path to the lake, considering possibilities and consequences. What should she do next? Sit tightly, and do nothing? Fly to Zurich? Although heading to Switzerland was her first choice, she didn't relish dealing with people whom she didn't want to see—namely Harold. Even though they still worked together on discreet business deals, he was still an ass. That said, she considered the risk may be worth it—she could keep an eye on her investigator as well as her ex-husband.

As she approached the shore, she immediately noticed her favorite chair, much worse for the wear. A few patches of chipped, turquoise paint struggled to retain their dignity, its wood weathered beyond repair. Sitting on it probably posed a threat to life and limb, but she didn't care—she sat gingerly, making certain it would hold her weight, then gazed across the lake. Ice adorned its edges like vintage lace, a subtle warning of wintry days ahead.

If I'm going to make a move, she thought, *I have to do it now . . .* Fully realizing if her plan were to knock Colbie Colleen off her high horse, she sure as hell couldn't do it from the designer couches of her brother's estate. Doing so made her feel disconnected. Out of touch. And, if she were honest with herself, all she had to rely on were sporadic updates from Harold, and he wasn't exactly being a chatterbox about what was transpiring in Zurich. Not only that, she knew him well enough to know he would tell her only what he thought was important, and little else.

Then, as the sun dipped behind distant trees across the water, her thoughts turned to Reginald. Her one and only sibling. *You were weak, dear brother—and, you refused to see what was in front of you. Everything would have been fine!*

And, there she sat. As fading filaments of light turned to shadows, Nicole Remington made her decision.

It was the only thing she could do.

****

Two men emerged from the limo, scanning the area in each direction as their boss exited and stood for a moment, attaché in hand, making sure his coat, hat, and gloves were just so. He turned to the man who, in the right costume, could pass for Bigfoot. "Time?"

"Eight-thirty . . ."

"Perfect—I'll be back in fifteen minutes. If I'm not, wait in the lobby for ten minutes. Anything after that, take action." He knew he didn't have to repeat the usual directions, but he preferred to cover all bases. A screw-up because of inefficiency? Unacceptable. Fischer strode toward the front door, not waiting for his security guard's affirming nod.

Without seeming obvious, he scanned the bank lobby—no one. Employees were long gone, and only those committed to making it to the top were on different floors, wading through mounds of paperwork. That's the way it always was and, within minutes, his contact would appear, showing him to a private office known only to those who could truly affect the institution's bottom line.

And, their personal pocketbooks.

"Gaspar! How good to see you! Right on time!" The slightly built man shook Fischer's hand enthusiastically, gently guiding him to a cubby of private elevators, out of sight from—well, no one.

Fischer retracted his hand as quickly as possible, fearing a lingering handshake could be a catalyst for illness, and it was his personal preference to always wear gloves—except in private, of course. "Mr. Bruder! It's good to see you, as well!"

Both men played their parts beautifully in case of prying eyes, and it wasn't until they stepped into the elevator, its door fully closed, before the conversation turned to business.

"I trust everything is in order?" Fischer gripped the attaché a little tighter.

"Indeed—as always . . ."

The elevator doors opened silently, Bruder exiting first. "Please—come with me . . ."

The room was soundproofed, no cameras. Completely private, business transactions were negotiated and agreed upon without fear of discovery and, most important, there was money to be made—for everyone.

Fischer placed the attaché on the teakwood conference room table. "I'm sure you understand—but my time is limited. Shall we proceed?"

Bruder presented a long, slender, Kevlar case. "This is representative of each . . ." He opened it, waiting for Fischer's response.

"We're agreed this is partial payment, yes? Upon approval, we'll consummate our agreement . . ."

"Understood." Bruder closed the case and locked it, handing it to Fischer as his other hand grasped the attaché.

Without word, Gaspar Fischer retraced his steps, Bruder at his side until they reached the heavy front doors. "Until next time," he advised, pulling on his gloves before Bruder had a chance to offer his hand for a germ-ridden shake.

"Indeed, Mr. Fischer—until next time . . ."

****

"Did you get ahold of Jan Bachman," Brian asked from behind the wine menu.

"Only his office—the secretary told me he's out for the next week—traveling, she said . . ."

"You sound as if you don't believe her story . . ." Brian laid the menu on the table. "The usual? Merlot?"

Colbie nodded. "The sooner the better! This has been a long, long day . . ."

Brian grinned, reaching for her hand from across the table. "How long?" He couldn't resist teasing her—he knew his lame jokes always made her laugh.

It worked. Colbie chuckled, her fingertips meeting his in the middle. "Well—maybe it wasn't that long!" She paused for a minute, thinking about the numbers four, seven, and eight. "Unless I can get personal interviews with these guys, we're at a standstill . . ."

"By now, I imagine word is beginning to circulate you're snooping around—especially since you don't trust Gaspar Fischer as far as you can throw him . . ."

"I don't trust him—so, since he's our only lead right now, it's my thought we should keep him in sight."

"As in surveillance?"

The waiter arrived, presenting their bottle of wine. Brian nodded at Colbie, both waiting for the pour—and, for the waiter to disappear.

"Exactly—as in surveillance." She took a sip, and closed here eyes. "I feel better already!"

Brian laughed, holding his goblet up for a toast. "To long days—and, making them better!" He took a sip, then placed his glass on the table. "When do you want to start?"

"Tomorrow . . ."

"Okay—I'm down . . ."

Colbie leveled a serious look. "There's something really bothering me, though . . ."

Brian recognized the tone—she had something serious to discuss. "About Fischer?"

"No—Nicole Remington." She paused, subconsciously tapping the base of her wine glass with her index finger. "What if I'm wrong?"

"Wrong about what?"

"Her—veracity."

There it was again. Self-doubt. *What the hell's going on with her,* he wondered as he studied her face. "I'll tell you what doesn't make sense to me—you're always right. Well, at least for the most part—and I don't understand why you're doubting yourself all of a sudden . . ."

"I'm not doubting myself—but, I think it's something we have to consider. What if I'm wrong about Nicole? What if she's out to get me?"

Brian grinned. "Out to get you? Like in a personal vendetta? You're kidding, right?"

Colbie dabbed at her lips with a starched, white napkin. "No—I'm not . . ."

Brian sat back in his chair. "Well, maybe you're right—maybe we should consider your being wrong about her. But, let me ask you—have you had any visions leading you in that direction?"

"No . . ."

"Have you heard something about her that has you spooked?"

"No . . ."

"Then, what? Unless you have a concrete reason for doubting Nicole, I think you're on the wrong track . . ." Brian couldn't believe he was actually defending Remington.

Colbie sighed, relief evident as her shoulders relaxed. "You're probably right—I think I would have sensed something if she's playing me for a fool . . ."

Brian raised his glass again. "That's my girl! You're good, and you know it!"

Colbie met his toast.

Am I?

****

Snow began to fall toward the end of the day—just when Colbie and Brian decided to head back to Gruyères.

"Don't you think it's a little late? Maybe we should wait until tomorrow . . . ." Brian shot Colbie a hopeful glance.

"I know the weather sucks, but I'm hearing a voice telling me to go . . ." Colbie pulled on hiking boots, and grabbed her parka. "You can stay here if you want . . ."

"Stay here, my ass! One, I'd never get over the self-imposed guilt and, two, you need me . . ."

"I need you?" Colbie belted out a gut laugh as she handed Brian his gloves.

"That's right—you need me!"

"How about if we discuss it in the car?" She opened the door with a sweeping gesture. "Shall we?"

Twenty minutes later they hit the outskirts of town, the two-hour drive to Gruyères giving them plenty of time to discuss the particulars of the case. "Have you thought more about Nicole?" Brian knew Colbie well enough to know if there were something still bothering her, it was best to place all cards on the table.

"No, not really." She hesitated. "Well—kind of . . ." Colbie stared out the window, frosty countryside whipping by without her knowing.

"Tell me . . ."

She turned to him, adjusting her coat so it didn't bunch up. "There's a part of me that thinks I jumped into this case too fast—I didn't do a comprehensive background check on Nicole since she got out."

"Why do you think that makes a difference?"

"It may not make a difference, but I have an unsettling feeling things aren't what they seem . . ."

"But you know she was in prison for five years—this is her first year out. What more do you need to know?"

Colbie pulled off her mittens. "I'm not sure . . . but, mark my words—we're going to see Nicole Remington sooner than we think . . ."

****

It's true—death waits for no one. A small group of mourners huddled together beside the open grave, two dabbing their eyes. Snow was accumulating, and the smart thing would have been to march right back to Zurich—but Colbie refused to go. "Let's see this out," she suggested as they watched the graveside service from across the street. "Thirty minutes . . ."

With their car parked discreetly out of sight, Brian tried to inconspicuously surveil the service with binos, keeping an eye specifically on the pastor. He seemed innocent enough—a small man, although he could only see him from the back—and Brian wondered what makes someone act on religious calling. "Do you have the name of the pastor," he asked Colbie as he adjusted the binoculars.

"No—I tried Googling it, but nothing came up. Although, I have to say—a church of this size? It doesn't really seem a candidate for a website . . ."

"Good point—hey, check it out! The service is over . . ."

Three women dressed in black slowly made their way to the street corner where they hugged each other then went their separate ways.

And, that was that—someone's life came to an unceremonious close, and few cared.

"Let's wander over there—it's tacky to ask questions, but both of us might be able to tune in as we linger at the cemetery . . ."

Brian looked at her as if she were nuts. "Don't you think we'll be a little less obvious if we hang here?"

Suddenly, Colbie sat up straight, her eyes glued to the cemetery. The pastor shook hands with one of two men remaining by the grave, then disappeared around the corner of the church. "Look!"

Brian focused the binos, whistling softly as he honed in on a man stepping from the shadows of a small building at the back corner of the cemetery. "Hey—wait a minute! He looks familiar . . ."

"Damned right he looks familiar—that's Gaspar Fischer!"

****

"Well, well, well—if it isn't the lovely Nicole Remington. Unfortunately, I can't say you look younger every day . . ."

"Shut up, Rifkin—I didn't come here for a commentary on my skin care regimen . . ." She sat across from him, refusing to let him get the best of her. She could care less about his social graces—what she needed from him was his take on the best way to get to Colbie Colleen.

Really get to her.

Rifkin met her eyes, a stiff smile on his lips. "Impressive, Nicole—it seems your time in the hoosegow did you some good . . ."

"Perhaps—but, let's cut the crap. I'm guessing you know why I'm here . . ."

Rifkin shifted his legs, chains clanking against the bare metal of his chair. "Oh, I know why you're here. Let me guess—Colbie Colleen."

"Correct—what do you know about her that I don't know? And, don't give me any crap . . ."

"What do you have to offer?"

"Offer?" Nicole laughed, completely amused by his question. "Nothing—just remember I have a bit of information you'd hate to divulge . . ."

Rifkin's eyes narrowed. "Are you threatening me?"

"Threatening you? I wouldn't dream of it . . ."

The jailer shifted his weight, acutely aware of the timbre of the conversation.

Nicole and Rifkin shared a look. "I'm afraid there's no way I can help you," he said. "Besides, you have the smarts to take care of the situation on your own . . ."

"So—that's it?"

"That's it . . ." He calmly called to the guard. "I'm done here . . ." As the jailer gripped his arm and guided him toward the door, Rifkin wondered how stupid Remington could be. *If she doesn't watch her back,* he thought, *Colbie will mop the floor with her . . .*

CHAPTER ELEVEN

❝ I knew it! I knew Gaspar Fischer has something to do with that cemetery!" Colbie clutched Brian's arm as she realized the enormity of what they were witnessing.

"What do you think he has to do with the funeral?"

"Not a damned thing—remember I told you the first time we were here something felt like a lie?"

Brian nodded, carefully adjusting the binos' focus. "I remember—I felt the same way . . ."

"There's something going on—and, I know damned well Fischer's involved!" Colbie watched as the men rounded the corner of the church. "We better head out—if he gets wind we're on to him . . ."

"10-4 . . ." Brian handed her the binoculars, fastened his

seatbelt, and got the hell out of there.

Neither spoke as he negotiated the snow-covered streets. Colbie wasn't sure what to say—she couldn't quite wrap her brain around what they watched for the better part of forty-five minutes—was the funeral service the real deal? Or, bogus. Was there another reason Gaspar Fischer was there? Of course, there was a possibility he knew the deceased, but chances of that were slim. *And, why did he stay in the shadows?*

Finally, as they pulled onto the main road back to Zurich, Brian glanced at her. "So—what are you thinking?"

She didn't answer right away. "I think Gaspar Fischer, Harold Remington, and Nicole are in cahoots . . ."

"What? If that's the case, what's the game?"

Colbie sighed, her frustration evident. "That's the thing—I don't know. All I know is I can go back to a couple of my visions, but they're not really telling me much . . ."

"Which visions?"

"Well—remember before we came to Switzerland, and I had a vision of Heidi, and automatic weapons lined up on a table?"

"Yeah . . ."

"So—we figured out the Heidi thing. She represented Switzerland—but, we haven't figured out the weapons part of it . . ."

Brian slowed as they reached the perimeter of the city, turning toward their hotel. "I don't know, Colbie—weapons just don't fit this case. What would Nicole Remington have to do with weapons?"

"You got me—but, I'm certain Nicole is playing me for a fool. That means this case just took a one hundred and eighty degree turn—it's a whole different ballgame when our client becomes part of the investigation . . ."

****

She couldn't wait to kick off her shoes, and soak in a hot bubble bath. Brian ordered room service, and she had just enough time to release the kinks in her back.

"For me?" Colbie opened her eyes to see a hand holding a hot toddy.

"Yep—room service won't be here for a while, so enjoy the time you have to yourself . . ."

She smiled as she wrapped her hands around the steamy mug. "You spoil me . . ."

"I hope so—you deserve it!"

With that, he closed the door gently behind him, leaving Colbie to her thoughts. He noticed her escalating stress, and it was something he didn't give much credence—until he got the feeling she was doubting herself. And, it wasn't just about her not knowing what her visions were trying to tell her. No—her confidence was dipping in all facets of her life.

Colbie heard Brian turn down the television as she began to drift into her intuition. Usually, symbols formed immediately—that evening, however, she felt as if she had to coax them by asking pointed, pertinent questions.

What does Gaspar Fischer have to do with the cemetery, she mentally asked her spiritual guide. She waited for a symbolic answer, her body relaxing further into the warm water and bubbles. Suddenly, her mind exploded with brilliant visions—a casket. A headstone. A comedy-tragedy mask. Colbie felt her body tense as she tried to figure out their meanings, but nothing was obvious. Of course, the casket and headstone could represent the cemetery, and nothing else—but, she didn't think so. Usually, her visions didn't repeat merely to corroborate a preexisting vision— each symbol had its own specific meaning. The comedy-tragedy mask? She had no idea.

Realizing she needed to relax, she asked another question after clearing the symbols by mentally wadding them up and throwing them away—it was a system she used for years. Her mind swirled like a pinwheel, the question she was about to ask the most important—*is Nicole Remington involved?* Without warning, her body convulsed, writhing in the bathtub as if an invisible person were pulling her legs, trying to make her drown. She fought to regain her composure, fully aware of the symbols forming, then splintering in her mind. A contorted face loomed in front of her, its intent to scare the livin' crap out of her.

It worked.

Holy shit! What was that? Her body trembling, she crawled from the tub to wrap herself in a heated bath towel. Legs barely supporting her, she collapsed onto the toilet, her body sapped of all energy. "Brian!" Nothing. "Brian!" She heard him running toward her.

"Colbie! Colbie! Are you okay?"

She nodded.

"What the hell happened?"

She could barely speak, her face blanched with fear. After a few moments, she looked at him. "Nicole Remington is our enemy—I was right . . ."

Brian squatted in front of her, eyes meeting hers. "I'm not sure what you're talking about . . ."

Colbie hung her head, wrapping the towel tighter. "She's evil . . ."

Brian recognized Colbie's state of mind—and, body. He saw it once before when her visions were particularly vivid. "Tell me what you saw . . ."

As Colbie recounted her experience, she cried softly as she told him of her terrifying vision when she asked about Nicole Remington. "Why the hell can't I get it together? What's wrong with me?" Colbie broke down, sobs taking charge of her body.

Brian listened, trying to process what she was telling him. If correct, Nicole Remington presented a monumental danger to anyone involved in the case.

"C'mon—let's get you off the toilet, and onto something more comfortable . . ." She allowed Brian to help her, and moments later she was safely on the couch in front of the fireplace, wrapped in her bathrobe.

"Hot chocolate? I'm having one . . ."

"How about another small toddy?" She managed a wan smile, still trying to erase the image associated with Nicole from her mind. "You realize what this means, don't you," she called to him as he wrestled with the milk carton.

"Well, I'm not sure I understand all of it, but the toddy and hot chocolate will be done in a minute—let's wait to review it until we're both comfortable and open to what you saw . . ."

Colbie smiled. *Open to what I saw? How times change . . .*

Within minutes, they settled in, ready to discuss Colbie's visions. The case. What to do next. "Let's tackle everything one-by-one—Nicole first?"

Colbie nodded, struggling to bring the vision to the forefront of her mind. "I have to tell you—I've never felt or seen anything like it, and it scared me to death!"

As she lifted the cup to her lips her fingers trembled, and Brian thought she resembled a small child, ready to take whatever punishment her parents would dish out—and, it was in that moment he realized how fragile she truly was. "Okay—walk me through it. Why do you think Nicole is involved?"

Colbie looked at him. "I think Nicole, Harold, and Gaspar Fischer are in cahoots . . ." She paused for a moment, thinking about her vision. "I also think Nicole hired me for a specific purpose . . ."

"Which is?"

"To take me down . . ."

"That can mean a bunch of things—take you down, how?"

"I think she wants me dead—and, she has the contacts to make it happen."

Brian tried to keep his cool as he thought of Nicole

Remington's kidnapping him, then shackling him to a chair. "If that's the case . . ."

"It is the case—I'm sure of it!"

Both sat quietly, the implications staggering. Brian fumed while Colbie began to strategize. "What she doesn't realize," Colbie commented, "is now that I know? It's game on . . ."

"What are you going to do?"

"For starters, I'll play it her way—for a while. That gives me time to figure out how I can land her in prison for the rest of her life—she better get ready because I'll mop the floor with her!" As soon as the words left her lips, Rifkin's face appeared in her mind's eye. *That's weird*, she thought. *Does he have something to do with this?*

Brian grasped Colbie's hand, giving it a squeeze. "That's my girl—anything you need from me . . . well, you know you have it. It won't hurt my feelings any to slap her ass in jail . . ."

As much as both of them wanted to talk more about it, they didn't have the energy—both were spent, and a good night's sleep seemed best.

Brian helped her up from the couch, making sure she was steady on her feet. "You know I love you, don't you?" He pulled her close, feeling her fear fade as he wrapped his arms around her.

"I do—I really do . . ."

****

Truth be known, she hated the last vestiges of fall, no matter how glorious the leaves. Ever since she could remember, winter was the season to stay inside sipping hot chocolate, sitting in front of the fire. It wasn't for flying halfway around the world to a country where winter was as fickle as a cheating man—or, woman.

As she exited the airport to a waiting limo, stinging rain slapped her face much like Reginald did when they were in their teens—she didn't like it then, and she didn't like it now. In fact, that little scene caused quite a ruckus in their family, and Nicole distinctly remembered her brother getting in a boatload of trouble for it. "It's unbecoming," his mother admonished. "And, we—as Champagnes—are above such low-brow actions . . ." Of course, there was punishment for what he did—she took away Reggie's car for a day. A whole twenty-four hours, hoping he would change his ways. For the life of them, Nicole's parents couldn't figure out why their darling boy was becoming such—well, an ass. They didn't like the changes they witnessed, but there was, apparently, nothing they could do about it. The weird thing was no one else noticed his morphing from a nice young man to an arrogant shit who thought he was better than everyone else. No—he played the game well as his duplicitous nature began to emerge.

After she slipped into the plush passenger's seat, the limo eased into traffic, it's driver at her beck and call with specific instructions. First, her hotel—she would take no more than thirty minutes to freshen up, and he was to wait for her return. Second, Harold's office—he, of course, had no idea she was going to descend on him in a raging fury, and she relished the idea of embarrassing him, as well as making him feel unprepared and uncomfortable. She knew damned well he was keeping things from her—things pertaining to her livelihood—and she wasn't going to have any part of it. After all, she was in charge—and, it didn't bother her in the least she was prepared to throw her weight around.

There was a slight problem with that approach, however—Harold never accepted she was in charge of their partnership, and he refused to treat her as equal. He never thought of his ex-wife as someone who could back him into a corner, and he wasn't about to let that happen. In fact, Harold didn't have any idea Nicole's plans far exceeded their mutual Zurich connections.

The driver waited in front of one of the swankiest hotels in Zurich as directed and, within thirty minutes, Nicole appeared, ordering him to drive her to the financial district. She debated having him wait for her, but finally decided she would send him on his way. With no idea of how long her conversation with Harold would take, she figured it more prudent to play it by ear. Besides, she could grab a quick bite to eat afterward, and she didn't want to feel as if she had to hurry because of a waiting limo driver—not to mention the cost.

The driving rain did little for her mood and, by the time she strode though the door to Harold's office, she was ready for battle. "Don't bother to announce me," Nicole ordered Monique as she made her way to the inner office.

"But . . ." Monique took off her glasses, immediately intimidated by the woman she'd never seen before.

Nicole ignored the weak rebuttal with a dismissive wave, opening the door to Harold's office without knocking.

"What the . . ."

"Surprised to see me, Harold?" She loved seeing him in a weakened position—it made her business with him easier.

Harold sat momentarily, quickly figuring out how best to handle the situation without alerting his staff there was a problem—that was the last thing he needed.

"Nicole—what the hell are you doing here?" He remained seated, clear his action would telegraph he had no respect for her.

"Is that any way to greet your business partner?" Nicole thought she noticed small beads of sweat forming on his forehead.

Harold tried to recover quickly from the shock of seeing her, but his effort was clumsy and ineffectual. "Why are you here—I don't recall having a conversation about a visit . . ."

"That's because there wasn't one. No—I thought it would be much more fun to arrive unannounced . . ."

"That doesn't answer my question—what are you doing here?"

Nicole made herself comfortable in a chair across from his desk. "We have business to discuss . . ."

Harold studied her for a moment, realizing he would have to tread lightly. When Nicole was in a mood, there was no reasoning with her. "And, what business would that be?"

His ex-wife flashed a knowing smile. "You know—the product . . ."

Just as she was about to launch into a diatribe about his ignoring her, as well as lying about business profits, Gaspar Fischer dramatically threw open the door, waltzing into Harold's office as if he owned the place, instantly recognizing he may have walked into a hotbed of contention. "Nicole! How lovely to see you!" He glanced quickly at Harold, then back at Nicole.

"Gaspar—how fortuitous! I was just about to discuss business with Harold—do you care to join us?"

That didn't sound good. Gaspar Fischer wanted nothing to do with difficulties between Harold and Nicole, and he had no intention of getting caught in the middle.

"I'm afraid I can't . . ." He checked his watch. "I have an appointment in twenty minutes . . ."

Nicole shot him a look that would have shriveled the staunchest of men. "How unfortunate—perhaps we can get together before I return to the States . . ."

Gaspar smiled. "That will be lovely—shall I be in touch?" Of course, Fischer had no intention of calling her for a meeting, and he immediately started planning an impromptu business trip.

"Not necessary, Gaspar—I'll call you when I'm ready to see you . . ."

Ready to see me? Who the hell died, and left you boss? "That will be fine . . ." He focused on Harold. "I'm sorry to intrude—Harold, will you please give me a call when you have an extra minute?"

A sour look flickered across Harold's face. "My calendar is full until late tomorrow afternoon—can it wait?"

"Of course—no hurry. I just thought I'd pop in while I was in the area." Again, he focused on Nicole. "Please forgive me for interrupting . . ." With that, he eased out the door, closing it softly behind him.

Nicole leveled a look at her ex-husband. "Well—Gaspar's interruption was fortuitous. For you, I mean . . ."

It was then Harold lost his cool, a darkness filling his eyes. "Get on with it, Nicole—then, get out. I don't have time for your games . . ."

"Oh, it's not a game, Harold—in fact, I think once you hear what I have to say, you may be a little more gracious to your dear, ex-wife . . ."

"I doubt it . . ." Harold got up, heading to the teakwood bar at the far side of his office—he was sure he was going to need a drink. He didn't however, offer Nicole one—the less time he had to spend with her, the better.

Nicole watched as he poured a single-malt scotch, neat. "It seems you're being less than honest . . ."

Harold turned, leaning against a massive bookcase to the right of the bar. "What does that mean? Less than honest about what?" He wasn't about to tell her or discuss anything until he knew why she thought she could push him around.

"Numbers, Harold—numbers . . ."

CHAPTER TWELVE

" Please—allow me to lock up . . ." The diminutive pastor quickly headed for the heavy, wooden door, key in hand. Moments later, he again stood with his guest. "Shall we?" He glanced at the door, even though he knew it was locked.

"Indeed—I trust you have everything ready to go?"

"I do . . ." The pastor led the way, unlocking a small door leading to the basement of the tiny church. "Watch your step, please—we had a slight plumbing problem a couple of weeks ago, and we still suffer its ill effects . . ."

The man ignored him.

At the bottom of creaky, wooden stairs, the pastor switched on a light, illuminating a dank, dark room furnished with only one table—on it, lay a long, slender, Kevlar case.

"Open it . . ."

The pastor took his position on one side of the table, his guest on the other. Carefully, locks facing away from him, the pastor opened the case, sliding it slightly toward his guest.

"This represents the entire transaction?"

"I am told it does . . ."

The man studied the case's contents, assessing everything. "I am ready to conclude . . ." He set the attaché he carried on the table, sliding it toward the pastor. "I'm sure you'll find everything's in order . . ."

With the gentleness of offering a communion wafer, the pastor flipped the locks, and opened the case. "Excellent— are you prepared for delivery?"

The man nodded. "Of course—my men are waiting for my word . . ."

"Then, give it . . ."

****

"Nicole is in Zurich . . ."

Brian looked up from his laptop screen, peering at Colbie over his glasses. "What did you just say?"

"I said Nicole is in Zurich . . ."

"How do you know that? Did you talk to her?"

"No—but I know."

Brian set his laptop on the table, joining her on the couch. "From when? How long has she been here?"

Colbie looked at him, grateful he no longer dismissed her visions as a pile of crap. "She just arrived—no longer than twenty-four hours . . ."

"Do you have a handle on where she is?"

"She's moving—not staying in one place for long."

Both remained quiet, their thoughts going back to Colbie's episode in the bathtub. If what Colbie said were true, Nicole Remington's arriving in town signaled a turn toward a place neither Brian nor Colbie wanted to go.

"Do you know why she's here?"

Colbie closed her eyes, allowing her mind's eye to spring to life—instantly, she saw four hands. As she watched, the hands moved over two cases on a table.

"Business—but, I don't know what business . . ."

Brian allowed her time to view her visions as if they were movies—interrupt her now, and that could be the end of any information she may see.

"And, me—us."

Brian immediately knew she was referring to her recent visions about Nicole's true reason for hiring her. "Us? I'm included in it now, too?"

Colbie opened her eyes. "It seems so, but I didn't recognize that before—she holds both of us responsible for ruining her life . . ."

"Oh, c'mon! She bought that train ticket all by herself— the idea to kidnap me didn't come from either one of us!"

"But, we ruined the plan—we're responsible for sending her to the slammer."

Again, they sat in silence. Finally, Brian took off his glasses and rubbed his face, small bits of hair spiking up as he ran his fingers through it. "So—now what? What's next?"

"I'll call Nicole first thing in the morning, talking as if I think she's stateside. I'll bring her up to date on what we know so far, as well as let her know I have an appointment with law enforcement here." Colbie paused, thinking through her plan. "In other words, I'll act as if I'm carrying on with the case—she'll never suspect we're on her ass now."

Brian considered Colbie's plan, trying to think of things that could possibly go wrong. They couldn't risk tipping their hand, and he wanted to make sure Colbie thought of everything.

Sometimes, she didn't.

"Okay—but you have no idea of where she's staying. That's going to make surveillance a little tricky . . ."

"True—but, I have an idea of where to look. I think she's staying in Zurich and, when I picture it, the hotel appears to be older architecture. White . . ." Again, she closed her eyes. "It has spire-looking things on the top—on the corners."

"I know that place! We passed it on the way to our hotel when we arrived!"

"Then that's where we start . . ."

"Tomorrow?"

"Yep—we need to know where she goes, and who she sees. I know she's up to her neck in something illegal—nefarious—but, I can't figure out what it has to do with Reginald's death . . ."

"Maybe," Brian surmised, "the Reggie thing is nothing but a ruse. Maybe it was a way to get you to Zurich . . ."

Colbie looked at Brian, eyebrows arched. "You think?"

"Well, it makes sense to me. She's smart enough to know how you think, and I'll bet she figured—at some point in our investigation—you'd have to fly to Switzerland."

"Then she'd have me on foreign ground—no familiarity."

"Precisely—unfortunately, the one thing I can say with certainty is Nicole Remington isn't stupid . . ."

Colbie nodded. "That's for sure. I'll call Tammy first thing—before I talk to Remington—to see if she's heard from Nicole, or knows anything on her end."

"Nicole wouldn't tell her where she's going . . ."

"That's not what I mean—one of the reasons I love working with Tammy is she listens. She hears the nuances in our clients' voices, and she never hesitates to let me know if she feels something . . ."

Brian agreed. "You're lucky to have her . . ."

"I know—now, Nicole is in our sights. Twenty-four hour surveillance . . ."

"Do you want me to call Carl?

Colbie looked at him, a determined look on her face. "Yes—I asked him to stand by . . ."

****

"I can hardly hear you . . ." Once again, the connection between Zurich and the States was less than stellar. Weather moved in overnight and Switzerland's major city was blanketed in snow—and, even though it would melt by day's end, it was enough to throw a wrench into Colbie's and Tammy's conversation.

"I can't hear you well, either—it's the tunnel thing, again . . ."

Colbie tried to quell her frustration. So far, the Reginald Champagne case wasn't going as well as she hoped. If she couldn't get a handle on what was really going on, Nicole would wind up on the warpath—if she weren't already. That would make Brian and her considerably behind in the game. "That's okay—let's make the best of it—have you heard from Nicole?"

"Nada. I thought surely she would have contacted you by now . . ."

Colbie didn't like the sound of that—if Nicole Remington were running silent, it meant she was implementing a plan. Oh, it involved Colbie alright—just not in the way Remington indicated at the onset of the case.

"That's not good. Listen carefully, Tammy—I need you to review everything in Nicole's file, including all press articles regarding her time in prison. Research where she went, and who she saw since she got out, if you can . . ."

"Am I looking for anything in particular?"

Colbie paused, thinking back to Nicole's relationship with those who kidnapped Brian five years prior. "I'm not sure, but check to see if she visited Rifkin in prison . . ."

"Rifkin? Why would she go there?"

"Why, indeed . . ."

****

Dinner was late that night—neither felt like going out, so Colbie ordered room service while Brian stepped out for a bottle of wine. Since arriving in Zurich, her appetite was non-existent, and Brian was getting worried she was compromising her health. "Oh, for God's sake, Brian—I'm fine! Stop being such a mother hen . . ."

"Mother hen? That's an old one—can't you come up with something more contemporary?"

Colbie laughed as she thought of their conversation.

The sad thing was Brian was right—she had lost weight. So, that night she ordered prime rib, baked potato, and roasted asparagus for both of them—if that didn't slap on a pound or two, nothing would.

"Snowing again!" Brian held up a bottle of merlot as he closed the door to their room.

"I noticed . . ."

"I decided I'm not a snow kind of guy—give me a beach any day!" He laughed as he shook melting snow from his jacket.

"How about taking a trip after this case? Somewhere warm . . ."

"Sounds good to me—shall I start planning our itinerary?"

Minutes later, they sat on the couch, sipping the full-bodied wine. "Did you connect with Carl?" Brian hadn't worked with him before, but, from everything Colbie told him, Carl Jennings was the best when it came to 'round-the-clock surveillance.

"Yep—we'll take shifts. You and I will begin tailing Nicole tomorrow morning, and Carl will take the night detail." She focused on Brian, a serious look in her eyes. "I have a feeling this is going to get ugly . . ."

****

Nicole Remington didn't care about much in life—except revenge. She'd had it with being pushed aside, and having someone else in control of her life didn't sit well. Why would it? Ever since her split from Harold, everything went to crap, and she held her ex-husband, brother, and Colbie Colleen directly responsible. Alvin McGregor, too. If she hadn't met him or listened to his drivel about her being the most important person in his life, none of it would have happened.

Nonetheless, that was the past—or, it was supposed to be. If she had her way, she'd be living the high life on an island in the Caribbean—at least, that's what she planned for herself when Harold decided she was an albatross around his neck. Not only that, Nicole was certain he felt a sordid sense of delight when she was sentenced to prison, although he never verbalized it. Even though he was a creep, it was his style to recognize talking about her unfortunate incarceration would be in poor taste.

As she picked at her breakfast—two eggs, sausage, and an English muffin—her anger seethed as she thought of how Harold screwed her back then, and how he was still screwing her. For the past few years, she thought it was in her best interest to let him revel in the misconception of his being in charge. Now? Not any more. *Get ready, Harold*, she thought as she took a sip of coffee. *Your days of taking me to the cleaners are over . . .*

By the time the last sausage link was gone, her plan began to take shape. The first thing she needed to do was contact Jan Bachman—even though he was an important colleague of Harold's, Bachman didn't make any bones about the fact he wouldn't mind getting to know Nicole better. And, although he never acted upon it, she knew Bachman would be in her corner for anything she asked him to do.

In fact, she depended on it.

****

"You ready?"

Colbie nodded, slipping on her coat and gloves. "I talked to Carl—he'll take over tonight . . ."

"Did you fill him in on everything?"

"No—he doesn't need to know the particulars. All I need him to do is tail Nicole, and let us know where she is as well as what she's up to."

"So, I take it our first stop is the white hotel . . ."

"Yep—one thing I remember about Nicole is her propensity for getting up early. She's usually ready to go by seven . . ."

Brian checked his watch as he held the elevator door for Colbie. "It's almost seven now . . ."

"I know—good thing the hotel isn't far. Only five blocks, or so . . ." Colbie adjusted her scarf as frigid air of the Zurich morning stabbed at her. "The other thing I remember about Nicole is she doesn't like cold weather—if anything, today's temp will coax her to stay inside a little longer."

"I checked the map—there's a coffee shop across the street and, a few doors down, is a neighborhood bread place."

"Let's check out the bread shop—it'll have coffee, and we can plant ourselves out of sight. I don't want Nicole to suddenly feel as if she's being watched . . ."

"Is she a sensitive?"

"No—I just don't want to take any chances . . ."

Within a few minutes, they opened the door to a bread bakery that smelled as good as a roasting turkey on Thanksgiving morning. "Oh, Brian—look at this!"

Brian grinned as Colbie took a deep breath, committing to memory the fragrance of freshly baked bread and strong coffee. "It's like stepping back in time, isn't it?"

Colbie nodded, scanning the bakery from front to back. "No kidding . . ."

Wicker baskets filled with breads, scones, and muffins lined the shelves, some still warm from the oven. By the front door was a refrigerated case for an assortment of cheeses and, toward the back, a small coffee bar. "What's your fancy," Colbie asked as she peered at the cheese. "A nice wedge of Brie this early in the morning?"

Brian laughed, and took her coat. "Maybe not—coffee and a scone is just fine . . ."

"Same here—we'll have to come back, though, to get cheese and bread to munch on this evening . . ."

A young woman greeted them and, a few minutes later, they headed to a table by the window, breakfast in hand. Before they could enjoy their first bite, however, Colbie grabbed Brian's hand. "Whoa! There she is!"

He checked his watch. "Right on time, too." For a split second, they looked at their breakfast, then at each other. "Hurry!" They grabbed their coats, coffee, and scones keeping their eyes glued on Nicole Remington—lose her now, and they'd have to wait until she returned.

By the time they made it out the door, Nicole was rounding the corner, heading straight for the financial district. "It's odd she's not taking a cab," Colbie commented.

"Maybe she isn't going far . . ."

Colbie watched as Nicole disappeared into a restaurant on the fringe of the district. "You're right . . ."

Brian kept an eye on her, too, taking mental note of pedestrians on the street. "Damn it! We can't go in there—too much risk of being recognized . . ." They stood at the corner, two doors down from the quaint breakfast bistro. "Do you think she's meeting someone, or she's just in the moody for a hearty breakfast?"

Colbie closed her eyes. "She's meeting someone . . ."

"Any idea who?"

She tuned in for a closer look. "Maybe—I'm not getting a clear vision . . ."

Both stood on the corner, figuring out what to do next. "I say we hang out here," Brian suggested, "and wait for her to leave. Maybe she'll leave with someone . . ."

"I doubt it—she's not that stupid."

"Do you have a better idea?"

Colbie looked at him, then back at the restaurant door. "Not really . . ."

So, that was it. Decision made. For the next hour they hung out at the corner, waiting for Nicole. It was worth the wait, too—a few minutes before eight, she pulled open the door, adjusted her coat and scarf, then headed deeper into the district followed by a bull of a man in a leather jacket. "Check it out! Do you think they were together?" Colbie's excitement mounted as she thought of another possible break in the case. She couldn't be sure, but she thought she recognized the man who lagged behind Remington. "Look at him—doesn't he look familiar?"

Brian focused on the bulky, middle-aged man striding down the street. "I think you're right! Isn't he one of the guys we're supposed to investigate? If so, he looks different, somehow . . ."

Colbie and Brian trailed Nicole and the man, hoping to get a better look. "You're right! He *is* one of the guys we're supposed to interview!"

"Which one?"

It was then everything fell into place. "I'm sure that guy is the seventh guy on our list!"

"Do you remember his name?"

Colbie thought for a moment, picturing the dossiers. "Jan Bachman! I'm sure that's it!"

They stepped it up to keep pace with Remington and, within minutes, she disappeared through the heavy doors to Harold's building.

Things were about to get interesting . . .

CHAPTER THIRTEEN

6 6 What did you find out?" For once, the connection to
Tammy was good, and they were taking the opportunity
to go over everything since Colbie had been gone.

"Well, not much. It appears Nicole Remington
disappeared off the face of the earth after she got out . . ."

"Nothing? Are you sure?"

"Pretty sure, although I did find out one thing . . ."

Colbie waited, knowing Tammy was enjoying dangling
the carrot. "Okay, okay! Enough! What did you learn?"

"Only that Remington made a stop at the prison—just
like you suspected—before she took off to parts unknown .

"What? How do you know?"

"Let's just say it pays to have friends on the inside . . ."

Colbie thought for a moment. Remington would likely visit one of two people—Rifkin or Alvin McGregor. Maybe both. "Who did she see?"

"Are you sitting down?"

"I am now . . ." Colbie pulled out a chair from the small desk beside the bed.

"Rifkin."

Colbie took a long breath. "Are you sure?"

"Oh, I'm sure . . ."

Although Colbie wasn't surprised, Tammy's news still hit her smack between the eyes. *Why would Nicole visit Rifkin? For information on me?* She sat, cell phone in hand, barely hearing Tammy's voice asking if she were still there. *That has to be it*, she thought. *But, what would Rifkin have to tell her she didn't already know?*

"Colbie?"

"I'm here—I had a feeling, but I wasn't sure. You just verified what I already figured was true . . ."

"Which is?"

"Nicole Remington has the guts to play me for a fool . . ."

"What? I'm not sure I know what you mean . . ."

Colbie motioned to Brian who just walked in the door. "I'll tell you later . . ."

****

"Do you have it? All of it?" Nicole again sat across from Harold, waiting impatiently for his answer. Of course, she was ready for a lie, but she thought her personal appearance might help persuade him to tell the truth—for once.

"What do you mean, 'all of it?'"

"Don't toy with me, Harold. You and I both know you haven't given me my share for years—unfortunately for you, however, those days are over . . ."

Harold Remington sat back in his chair, an impudent smile playing on his lips. "You can't possibly be threatening me . . ."

Nicole leveled a scathing look. "If you choose to think so—then, yes."

"Rather a risky move, don't you think?"

"Oh, please—for some reason, Harold, you think you're in charge of this operation . . ." Nicole paused as her words took root. "Obviously, a misguided misperception . . ."

Harold didn't move. He hadn't counted on Nicole's showing up—or, her brash behavior—and he wasn't about to allow her to make waves with anyone within their small group of colleagues. "It surprises me," he told her, "you're taking such an abrasive approach. What makes you think you haven't been receiving your share?"

Nicole chuckled softly. "As I told you before, Harold— the numbers." She paused, waiting for his response. "Clearly, you're surprised at my business acumen—what makes you think I haven't kept track of everything since day one?"

"I never underestimated you, Nicole. I know you better than anyone, and one thing I fully understand about you is you're a snake—or, perhaps, black widow might be a more appropriate moniker . . ."

Again, Nicole chuckled—something that irritated the crap out of Harold. "You can think whatever you want—the bottom line is I'm here to collect—everything."

Both sat silently, weighing the individual threats. Nicole knew if Harold were smart, he'd comply with her request—if not, stiff consequences were already in place, waiting to be carried out by a main player in the game. It was something she kept close to the vest—unbeknownst to him, those Harold regarded as unyielding compatriots were more than ready to make the best deal for themselves. Loyalty meant nothing in their line of business and, if he weren't careful, he'd experience their duplicity the hard way.

Harold shifted uncomfortably in his chair. "I see—well, then, I suggest we get down to work. How much are you expecting?"

Nicole smiled. "This time? Fifty-seven—half for you, half for me. I think that's fair, don't you?"

"Fair? That all depends—I have expenses I don't pass on to you . . ."

"Unfortunately, that's your problem—if you can't cut a better deal for yourself, that has nothing to do with me . . ."

Harold leaned back in his chair, tenting his fingers as he tried to assess what Nicole was up to. Something was up, and he couldn't quite figure out what it was. "Alright—I'll go along with your suggestion for now—but, don't get used to it."

Nicole laughed aloud, delighted at how easily he caved. She fully expected an argument, but there was something in his demeanor indicating he was playing her differently than usual. "Excellent—now, there's one more thing we have to discuss . . ."

"And, that is?"

Nicole's eyes turned dark with disdain. "Colbie Colleen. It's important you speak with her . . ."

"Who the hell is she?" It was always smart to play it as if he didn't know a thing.

"Surely, you remember—the investigator who broke the oil-real estate scam. If it weren't for her, I wouldn't have spent time in prison—I had everything set up to take down Rifkin should things have gone south, and she had to show up, sticking her nose where it didn't belong . . ."

Harold busted out a gut laugh. "Is that what this is all about? Flexing your muscles for personal revenge?" He paused, watching her carefully. "And, what does that have to do with me?"

"That's part of it—but I needed to get her to Zurich without raising suspicion, and hiring her to investigate my darling brother's death was the best way. And, as my dear ex-husband, it would have been a misstep if I didn't suggest she speak to you . . ."

"I don't suppose you gave any consideration to her finding out the real circumstances of Reginald's death . . ."

"Of course, I did—but it doesn't matter. She won't be alive long enough to make anything of it . . ."

Harold eyed her, recognizing something in his ex-wife he hadn't seen before—it wasn't an attractive trait, but he had to admit it was exciting. "Something tells me you're playing with fire . . ."

"Not really—now, where were we? Oh, yes—my share. I assume you have it?"

"With me? No . . ."

Nicole wasn't amused. "Of course, you do, Harold—I know you, and I'm insulted you considered I might fall for such a lame excuse . . ."

As Harold viewed it, he was in a precarious situation. If he gave her what she were due, he'd set a dangerous precedent—from that moment, Nicole would expect nothing but a full, complete payment. That was bad enough—but it wasn't the worst. As he glared at his ex-wife, it was obvious she changed over the years. She used to be compliant. Easy to control. Now? She had little patience for those who chose to take advantage of her. The fact she obsessed about effecting revenge on Colbie Colleen was evidence enough and, simply from the way she spoke and carried herself, Harold had no doubt she meant business.

Nicole didn't say a word—after all, the ball was in his court. She knew damned well he kept a safe stashed with cash in his office—she just didn't know where. And, she did find his saying he didn't have it with him more than insulting. She learned a lot about her darling ex-husband during their years of marriage—more than he probably knew. She always watched, mentally cataloging everything he did, as well as people he saw. There was little she didn't know about him, so his not having a hefty amount of cash always within reach was absurd. "Well? Do you want to rethink your answer?" Her eyes met his. "It'll be in your best interest, you know . . ."

Harold hesitated for a moment, then placed his index finger on a sensor pad under his desk. Within seconds, a drawer opened, and he withdrew a handful of bills. He counted it quickly, placed it in an envelope, then handed it to her with a smirk. "Fifty-seven—a pleasure doing business with you . . ."

Nicole smiled sweetly. "See how much better things go when we understand each other?" She accepted the cash, counted it—just in case—then carefully placed the envelope in her designer bag. "Until next time, Harold. How nice to see you . . ."

She stood, and Harold watched her put on her coat and gloves, then walk toward the door. "Don't think for a second you've won, you stupid bitch . . ."

She turned. "Oh, Harold—now you ruined everything. I thought we were getting along—didn't you?" She paused, refusing to break his gaze. "But, you just couldn't keep your mouth shut, could you?"

With that, she strode through the door with a heightened level of arrogance and self-confidence. *You always were foolish, Harold,* she thought as she passed Monique at her desk without so much as a nod of acknowledgment. *Once a fool, always a fool . . .*

****

"There she is!" Colbie peered around the corner from a building across the street, ready to bolt if Nicole turned in their direction.

"Why are you whispering?"

"Because . . . very funny!" Colbie shot him a teasing glare, then turned her attention back to their target. "Let's go!"

Nicole Remington turned a corner heading south two blocks from Harold's building, then disappeared through the doors of a narrow building crammed between two skyscrapers. Colbie stopped a half block behind her, unsure of the possibility of being seen if they moved closer. From her position, she could read the building address, relaying it to Brian so he could Google it.

"It's an apartment building . . ."

"Here? Smack dab in the middle of the financial district? It must be high rent . . ."

Brian kept reading his phone. "Apparently, there was some sort of dustup way back when, and the historical building is one of few managing to beat the wrecking ball."

Colbie tugged at his sleeve. "Let's cross the street—maybe we can get a better view if we can see through the doors or windows."

Within minutes, they stood directly across from the narrow building, and Colbie was right—they could through paned-glass windows, revealing a beautifully appointed lobby as well as a classically-dressed doorman.

"High rent, is right—but it doesn't make sense. It can't be where Nicole stays because she's at the hotel." Colbie paused and closed her eyes, allowing her intuitive mind to jump to life. "She's visiting someone . . ."

"Can you tune in on who?"

"Give me a sec . . ." Colbie was silent as the vision of the small bistro popped in, then out." "The guy from the bistro—from earlier this morning . . ."

"Bachman? Are you sure?"

"Oh, yes—I'm sure. I see Nicole Remington standing with him—and, I see two glasses of champagne. Full."

"They're drinking champagne?" Brian was entering notes in his phone as she spoke.

"No—the glasses stand by themselves . . ."

Brian waited until Colbie opened her eyes, taking a moment to adjust. "What do you think they mean?"

Colbie grinned, planting a kiss on his cheek. "Really, Brian? Champagne? It's obvious . . ."

Brian blushed. "Oh, yeah—Reginald Champagne. But why are you getting something about him when you're tuning in on Nicole and Bachman?"

"Good question—it can only mean Nicole and Bachman are involved in Reginald's death.

Somehow . . ."

CHAPTER FOURTEEN

———— ✦ ————

Carl Jennings pulled on the hotel's heavy doors, keeping a low profile as he made his way to the elevator. Doing so was his natural personality, and his ability to fly under the radar kept him out of trouble on more than one occasion. Colbie knew it, too. They went back a few years and, after working with her on a few tough cases, he knew she was the real deal. Throughout his years as an investigator, he worked with psychics on other cases, but, truthfully?

Not impressed.

But, Colbie Colleen was different, and he felt it the second he met her—she wasn't full of herself, and it was clear she wasn't guessing about what happened throughout their investigation. Her visions—though he was skeptical, at first—were always right on the money, and she was directly responsible for wrapping up a case that otherwise could have taken months.

The elevator rose silently to the seventh floor, its doors opening with a slight hiss to a man and woman obviously returning from a night on the town. Fortunately for Carl, they declined riding with him to the ninth floor, promising to catch a ride on the way back down. He nodded, the doors closed, and he was, once again, alone with his thoughts as he rose with nearly imperceptible movement to his client's floor.

His task was to surveil Nicole after Colbie and Brian passed the baton to him at seven o'clock the previous night—but, unexpectedly, the evening took a turn. Now, he had to explain it to Colbie and Brian, uncertain of what they'd think.

The elevator dinged, and Carl stepped into the hallway, glancing quickly at the numbers on the wall to make certain he was going the right way. Within moments, he stood in front of their door, considering how he was going to tell them it wasn't Nicole he wound up following . . .

It was Harold Remington.

****

The pastor stood by a newly-dug grave, muttering an unintelligible prayer, then shuffled into the church, quietly locking the door behind him. As a young man of religious calling, he never thought he would be in such a position—but, how was he supposed to live on such a meager stipend? Oh, he tried, but soon found out the allure of money was stronger than his desire to help those in need. He was to operate his parish—if you could call it that—but, he learned quickly running a church and tiny congregation had nothing to do with religion. As a pastor, what he wanted transformed into something he didn't recognize, and it appeared as if there were no way out.

Except one.

The stairs creaked as he carefully made his way to a room that could be described as nothing more than a giant dirt hole with a few rotting ceiling beams, and a door that could be compromised with one push. Standing in the doorway, he flicked on the light, then positioned the chair in the middle of the claustrophobic room, making certain it was just so.

It was time.

****

"After you closed up shop for the night, I kept an eye on things from two different positions—first, from across the street in case Nicole decided to make a night of it. Then, I hung out in the lobby—neither yielded anything." Carl, flipped open his spiral notepad, thumbing through the pages. "Up until about one in the morning, there wasn't any action . . ."

"Then what happened?" Colbie watched her investigator review his notes.

"Well, you're never going to believe this . . ."

"Try me . . ."

Carl hesitated, then eyed his clients. "Harold Remington showed up . . ."

"At one in the morning? That seems a little odd, don't you think?" Brian glanced at Colbie, watching her face as she digested the information.

"I think saying it's odd is an understatement . . ." Colbie's forehead creased as she considered the implications. "There's only one reason Harold would show up at her hotel at that time of night . . ."

"He didn't want to be seen . . ."

"Exactly!"

Brian nodded, turning his attention to Carl. "Did she meet him in the lobby?"

"Nope—their meeting must have been prearranged because he didn't stop at the desk . . ."

"Did he use his cell?"

"Bingo! That's exactly what he did—right after he entered the hotel, he made a call. Of course, I don't have proof it was to Nicole, but it makes sense . . ."

Brian agreed. "I can't think of a reason Harold would be at Nicole's hotel room at that time of night, other than to meet with her. The question is why . . ."

"I'll be right back . . ." Colbie shot a knowing look to

Brian, excused herself for a moment, then gently closed the door to the bedroom. She felt intuitive impressions making an appearance, and she preferred to be alone to interpret them. After the bathtub incident, she didn't trust herself to keep things together.

She lay on the bed, kicking her shoes off as she made herself comfortable. Feeling her body relax, she called on her intuitive senses to reveal only true and valid information—she would accept no other. Within moments, the familiar comedy-tragedy masks appeared, instantly dissipating as another vision took its place. She watched as Nicole and Harold Remington appeared in her mind's eye, together as if they were the society couple of years prior. *What? That doesn't seem right . . .*

Colbie remained still, allowing the vision to explode, then fade to black. Slowly, with conviction and confidence, another vision appeared, picking up where the vision of Harold and Nicole left off. *This is weird,* Colbie thought as she watched—usually, her visions were comprised of symbols—that time, however, it was like viewing a film in full, graphic color.

She watched as if she were a fly on the wall, the couple laughing and toasting each other as though they didn't have a discordant past. None of it made sense to Colbie, but she didn't have the time to figure it out—Brian and Carl were still in the living room and, unless she reappeared soon, Brian would think something was wrong. Seconds later, she brought herself out of meditation, and quickly ran a brush through her hair, freshening her lip gloss, "Sorry," she apologized, entering the room with a smile. "I needed a bit of time to myself . . ."

Both men understood. "Apology accepted. Did you come up with anything," Brian asked.

"That depends—all the visions were about Harold and Nicole, but they don't make sense . . ."

Brian glanced at Carl. "Let's hear it—maybe we can help."

Colbie sat on the couch beside Brian, then recounted the visions. "I think I get the comedy-tragedy mask thing—it represents Nicole's duplicity. We took this case based on a lie Nicole crafted, and it's morphing into something completely different."

"It seems to me," Carl commented, "Harold and Nicole might be renewing their relationship . . ."

"Or, they never had problem with their relationship in the first place . . ."

Well, that statement was enough to render everyone silent! *Could it be true*, each wondered privately as they considered the fractured society couple.

Brian was first to address the elephant in the room. "If that's true, this case is a sham. We figured Nicole purposely guided us to Zurich for a reason other than the case for which she hired us, and my gut tells me she's up to her neck in something illegal . . ."

"And," Colbie offered, "don't forget—I'm on her radar, and that's not good . . ."

"Are you sure about that? After your visions tonight, whatever is going on with Harold and Nicole, it may not have anything to do with you . . ."

Carl glanced at both of them. "I don't get it—you think Nicole set this gig up as a sham, and her real intention is to get to Colbie?"

Brian nodded. "We don't have proof of that, though—at this point, it's a working concept . . ."

Colbie thought for a moment. "Maybe—but, I still think Nicole carries a need for relentless revenge. The more I learn about this case, the more I don't know . . ."

"This is what I don't get," Brian interjected. "What the hell does Reginald Champagne's murder have to do with any of this?"

Colbie looked at both of them. "I think it boils down to two things—what if Harold and Nicole aren't really divorced? What if that were all for show?"

Brian glanced at Carl, then back at Colbie. "You said there were two things . . ."

Colbie took a deep breathe before answering. "What if Harold and Nicole murdered Reginald? If that's the case, why—and, for what purpose?"

****

Coffee and a bagel was just what Colbie needed the following morning. By the time their hotel door closed quietly behind Carl, it was the wee hours, and the whole idea of Nicole and Harold murdering Reginald took the case on a tangent they hadn't previously considered. But, the more they thought about it, the more it made sense. And, what about Nicole's possible revenge on Colbie? Well—that made sense, too.

"What I don't believe," Colbie commented as the waiter filled her coffee cup, "is Harold and Nicole having a good relationship—at least, until recently." She took a sip, then a bite of her bagel. "I think they hate each other's guts, but they need each other for some reason . . ." She paused. "I think they need each other because of business . . ."

"So, now that you had time to think about it, what do you think is really going on?"

Colbie swallowed, then patted her mouth with her napkin. "I think Harold and Nicole murdered Reginald— maybe not with their own hands, but they have blood on them, nonetheless . . ."

Brian put his cup down, considering Colbie's comment. "The old hit-man theory?"

"Maybe—but, I think it's a real possibility." She looked at Brian, grinning. "If that's what's going on, I find it a little disappointing . . ."

"What do you mean?"

"Oh, you know—greedy couple offs family member for untold fortune . . ."

Brian chuckled, giving Colbie a quick kiss on her cheek. "You're right—it's cheesy!"

"You know what else I think?"

"What's that . . ."

"I think the men on our list are involved . . ."

"Which ones?"

"Not all of them—only four, seven, and eight."

"Let's see—four is Gaspar Fischer, seven is Jan Bachman, and eight is . . ."

"Gregor Hoffer—he's the guy I haven't talked to yet . . ." Colbie placed her napkin on the table.

"Do you have any idea of how he's involved?"

"Nope—but he's next on our list to find out!"

****

As they passed the front desk on the way back to their room, Colbie glanced at one of several Zurich newspapers. "Brian! Look!" She grabbed the paper, staring at it in disbelief.

"Holy shit! Is that the same church I think it is?"He couldn't take his eyes off the headline as they walked toward the elevators—*Pastor Takes Own Life.*

"It is!" She pointed to the picture of the small, stone church. "See? There's the cemetery . . ."

Brian, too, recognized the church immediately. "It's kind of weird for a pastor to commit suicide, don't you think?"

Colbie nodded.

"Something about this doesn't hit me right—why would a man of God do himself in? Isn't that against everything they believe in?"

"Well—we saw him with Gaspar Fischer, and we know Fischer's complicit in this whole damned thing. And, because we saw him with the pastor at the cemetery, it's clear they weren't strangers . . ."

Brian looked at Colbie as the elevator door opened. "Do you think Fischer has anything to do with the pastor's death?"

"My best guess? Yes—he does. I agree with you—something isn't right . . ."

Brian looked at her, then the newspaper. "What are we going to do?"

Colbie stepped off the elevator at the ninth floor. "Now—we start playing hardball. I need to talk to someone with the local authorities—maybe I can find out what they're thinking about this case . . ." She pointed to the newspaper. "You, in the meantime, can take a trip to the church. Nose around—it's a crime scene, and you never know what you'll learn. Stay out of sight, though—it's not a long shot that Gaspar Fischer or one of his colleagues may be there. Remember—we still don't know Fischer's relationship with the pastor. It may well be it's completely innocent . . ."

"You know damned well it's not innocent . . ."

"True. But we aren't sure what we're looking for—yes, Fischer is probably involved in some way, but we don't have anything definite, and we need to lay our groundwork.

We need proof of something . . ."

CHAPTER FIFTEEN

———— ❖ ————

G regor Hoffer stood silently, watching, as the pastor's body was loaded into a morgue van, then whisked away for an autopsy. A few people lined the village street, whispering about the tragedy at the church, wondering how such a thing could happen in their community. "It's just not possible," a woman in blue whispered to her friend. "Not here. Not in Gruyères . . ."

The other woman could only nod, mesmerized by the scene in front of her.

Parked out of site, Brian watched from his car, training the binos on the man standing quietly on the corner, not taking his eyes off the church. *Who is this guy,* he wondered, as he transferred focus of the binoculars from spectator to spectator. *Colbie's going to want to see this . . .* He snapped a few pics with his phone, then resumed his surveillance. *Maybe he's tied in with Fischer . . .*

Of course, Brian had no way of knowing, but his thought wasn't a silly one. As the case stood, he and Colbie had to suspect everyone, and no one was safe from scrutiny. The man standing on the corner was no exception—he didn't speak to local authorities, or display any grief or concern.

He simply stood, watching.

Something was screwy, and Brian felt the hair on his arms stand at attention. As sure as he sat there, he knew the guy on the corner had something to do with the pastor's death—and, the more he tuned into it, the more he recognized the poor pastor didn't willingly do himself in.

No—there was something much darker at hand . . .

****

"Who is this guy?" Colbie flicked through the pictures of the man standing on the corner near the church—she couldn't see his face from the camera angle, but, she too, thought he was involved.

"I have no idea—but I get the feeling he's not a stranger there . . ."

"What makes you say that? He could be someone who knew the pastor, and is mourning his passing . . ."

Brian took the cell from Colbie, again looking at the pictures. "Maybe—but, with the feelings I got, I don't think so . . ."

"Describe them to me . . ."

He looked at Colbie, a serious look on his face. "I'm not sure, really—all I know is the hair on my arms stood on end, and I had a strong feeling there's more to the pastor's death than first thought . . ."

"You don't think he committed suicide?"

Brian paused before answering, then looked at his better half sitting beside him. "I'd bet my paycheck on it . . ."

****

"Nicole? It's Colbie!"

Nicole did her best to sound as if she were glad to hear from her. "Colbie! It's been a long time—I was beginning to think you ran into a bit of trouble . . ."

"No—everything's fine. I tried getting in touch with you a few times, and I had my assistant try from the States, but it was a no go . . ."

Nicole did her best to gloss over Colbie's veiled

admonition. "Well—tell me. What did you learn? I assume after all this time, you must have something . . ."

Colbie hesitated, thinking about how she would craft a story Nicole would buy—first, however, it was time to put her client on the spot. "Where are you? I have a feeling you're not in the States . . ." Colbie thought she heard a slight gasp.

"Not in the States? Wherever did you get that idea?"

"You know me—just a feeling . . ."

"Well, you're half right—I'm in the States, but I decided to get away for a while. My family has a cabin on a lake, and I figured I could use the down time. I'm sure you know how that is . . ."

Colbie laughed, hoping it sounded genuine. "I know exactly what you mean!" She paused, considering how far she should take the ruse. "So, I'm making sense of the list of names you provided, and I only have Gregor Hoffer left to interview." Of course, that wasn't quite the truth, but Colbie and Brian knew several names on the list represented pure fluff, and there was no reason to interview them. After the revelation of the numbers four, seven, and eight, she realized Nicole included the others only as a diversion. "I'm starting to get a good idea about who killed Reginald . . ." There. That ought to put the fear of God into her.

At least, it should have—Nicole chose to ignore Colbie's last statement, responding to something more benign. "Gregor Hoffer? I don't know him personally, but I know Harold does business with him frequently . . ."

Time to set the hook. "How do you know that? I thought you and Harold barely spoke . . ."

Nicole hesitated a fraction of a second too long— long enough for Colbie to recognize she was becoming uncomfortable with the conversation. "Colbie—I'd love to talk, but I have an appointment in less than an hour. If I don't leave now, I'll never make it on time—we'll talk later!"

Dead air.

Colbie looked at Brian, mobile still in her hand. "Gee—she didn't even say goodbye . . ."

"That was an awfully short conversation—what did she say?"

"Not much. But, It doesn't take a genius to recognize she didn't want to talk—especially when I told her I picked up on the fact she changed location, and I had a good idea of who offed Reginald."

Brian grinned. "I bet she didn't! Do you think she has any idea we're on to her?"

"Right now? I don't think so. But, as we said before, she isn't stupid, and I wouldn't be a bit surprised if she sets up a tail on us . . ."

****

"Oh, yes—Mr. Hoffer is expecting you . . ." The sturdily-built German woman offered what Colbie interpreted as a pained smile. Disappearing into an inner office, she returned moments later, gesturing to Colbie to follow. "He will see you now . . ."

Colbie rose, still stunned by the ease with which she scheduled the appointment. After weeks of chasing rejection, Hoffer suddenly put her on his calendar the day after she spoke with Nicole. Coincidence? Maybe—but Colbie didn't think so. "Thank you . . ." Colbie followed the woman, a taste of uncertainty in her mouth. As she entered Hoffer's office, it was impossible not to notice the minimal, austere style. Chairs for guests placed closely together punctuated the space, and the only other piece of furniture was a stark metal desk. No file cabinets. No bar. Nothing of interest.

Gregor Hoffer stood to greet her, shaking hands with the strength of a man twice his size. "Ms. Colleen—please, have a seat . . ."

Colbie smiled, carefully letting go of his hand before he caused significant pain. "Mr. Hoffer—I appreciate your taking the time to meet with me . . ." She sat, adjusting her position slightly on the uncomfortable chair. "You're a difficult man to get ahold of . . ."

"I'm afraid that's true—business waits for no one!" His accent was thick, but it was clear he had a solid command of the English language. "Now—what can I do for you?"

"Well—as you know from Nicole Remington, I'm investigating the death of her brother, Reginald Champagne." Colbie paused, watching his reaction closely.

"Actually, no—I haven't communicated with Nicole for quite a long time . . ."

"Really? I must have misunderstood . . ." She paused. "Anyway, if you'll be so kind, I'd like to discuss what you know about Reginald's murder. I assume you have some idea regarding who decided to end his life . . ."

Hoffer leaned forward, placing his forearms on the desk.

"Now, why do you think that?"

"Only because Nicole provided a list of names who might have information . . ."

"Well, I hate to disappoint you, but Reginald and I were business colleagues, and I was as surprised as anyone when I heard of his unfortunate demise . . ."

"Why do you think he was murdered?"

"I have no idea, but I can well assume it had something to do with . . . unsavory individuals with whom he did business."

Colbie's eyes met his. "Unsavory? Why would he be involved with someone like that?"

Gregor Hoffer smiled. "Ms. Colleen, in our line of business, it's unwise to trust anyone . . ." He returned her steely stare. "I'm sure you understand because I have no proof, it's not in my best interest to engage in conjecture. However, I will tell you this—it's not outside the realm of possibility to consider Reginald's circle of friends . . ."

"Do you think it had to do with his banking business, or something more—personal?"

Hoffer sat back, and checked his watch. "Honestly, I have no idea. With whom have you spoken regarding this matter?"

"Several people, really—actually, you're last on my list."

"And, what have you learned?"

Colbie thought for a moment before answering. His question clearly had a different motive other than making conversation—he was trying to ferret out exactly what she knew. Why? Because Nicole Remington needed to know in which direction the case was turning. She knew Colbie well enough to know after several weeks on a case, there was no way Colbie would know nothing—and, she also knew Colbie would take a back-door approach, learning what she needed to know without being obtuse.

"I'm afraid I can't discuss the particulars—I'm sure you understand."

"And, I'm afraid I have no more time . . ." Hoffer picked up the phone, buzzing his assistant. "Greta? Will you please show Ms. Colleen out?" Within moments, Greta appeared at the door, waiting for Colbie to join her.

Colbie stood, extending her hand. "Thank you for your time . . ."

Hoffer accepted the handshake, taking the opportunity to shake her hand with more force than usual—perhaps a subtle warning she should keep her nose out of his business.

Greta accompanied her to the main entrance of the office building. "Enjoy the rest of your day, Ms. Colleen . . ." With that, she made sure Colbie exited the building, then disappeared into an elevator.

Making sure she didn't attract attention, Colbie crossed the street, ducking into an unobtrusive coffee shop around the corner where she and Brian agreed to meet.

"Well—how did it go?" Brian saw her waiting at the light, and ordered a fresh latte for her, as well as a streusel muffin.

"As I expected—although he didn't own up to speaking recently with Nicole, it was obvious he was lying . . ." Colbie pulled out a chair, draping her coat over the back. "It's no mystery Nicole ordered him to make time for me . . ."

"Ordered?"

"Yes—ordered. She's driving the bus when it comes to Jan Bachman and Gregor Hoffer . . ."

"What about Gaspar Fischer? Where do his allegiances lie?"

Colbie took a sip of her latte, then wiped a small amount of foam from her lips with a napkin. "Oh, I think that's pretty clear—he's joined at the hip with Harold Remington . . ."

"Ah—I get it! Warring factions . . ."

Colbie nodded, picked a piece from her muffin, then popped it in her mouth. "This is really good . . ." She paused, swallowed, then directed her attention to Brian. "I have no doubt Gaspar Fischer takes direction from Harold—Bachman and Hoffer are lesser players to some extent, but Nicole is the one pulling the strings. Now, all we have to figure out is why, and why Reginald Champagne was eighty-sixed. The way I see it, everything boils down to money—pure and simple . . ."

They sat in silence for several minutes, each trying to connect the dots. "Who do you think is the main player," Brian asked.

"Nicole . . ."

****

They sat at the small table in their room, papers spread in all directions. Interviews concluded, they needed to make sure they weren't missing anything. "So—that's it," Colbie commented as she sat back, looking at pictures of those they knew were involved—somehow—in the murder of Reginald Champagne. "The only one whom we don't know much about is Bruder . . ." She glanced at Brian. "He was one of the first guys we interviewed, and you seemed to think he wasn't involved."

"Do you disagree?"

"I do—I get the feeling he's involved more than both of us think. That said, I don't think he's a main player . . ."

Both stared at the pictures of the five men, Nicole Remington heading their makeshift organizational chart. "All of this is going to be tough to prove," Brian commented. "We don't have evidence—only ideas . . ."

"I know—the first thing we need to do is get our asses back to that church. I know as sure as I'm sitting here, it's an important part of this puzzle . . ."

Brian glanced at his watch, then out the window. "It's still early—we can make it to Gruyères before dark. If we're lucky, no one will be nosing around—except us."

Colbie looked at him, then glanced outside. "I'm game— let's get the hell out of here!"

CHAPTER SIXTEEN

B rian was right. By the time they reached the church, the town was beginning to button up for the evening, a light snow falling. Visitors slowly vanished from the streets, making Gruyères seem like every other village outside the city—small and inconsequential. One of seven districts of the Canton of Fribourg, its population was just over a meager two thousand and, as street lamps flickered on, only the heartiest stock braved the frigid air.

Towering peaks framed the village as they parked away from the church, both thinking it prudent to be certain no one was there before getting a closer look at the cemetery. Since the pastor's passing, Colbie imagined the church was secure, but they couldn't take that thought for granted— especially since they knew Gaspar Fischer was involved somehow.

Colbie glanced up and down the street, then at the church. "This is kind of creepy—it doesn't feel the same."

"I know what you mean—something feels strange. But that's what we always say when we're here . . ."

"True—let's check out the cemetery one more time." She paused, thinking of the diminutive pastor. "Do you think he's is buried here?"

"Who?"

"The pastor—it seems likely he would be . . ."

Brian didn't answer for a minute. "I never thought of that—maybe. But, from here, it doesn't seem as though there are freshly dug graves . . ."

Colbie nodded. "That's what it looks like, but I want to get a closer look . . ."

Looking like a star-crossed couple, they walked hand-in-hand to the doors of the tiny church, Brian pulling on its ancient handles. "Locked. Let's see if there's another door 'round back . . ."

"Well—it makes sense there would be one, but let's check out the cemetery first . . ."

Backtracking down the snow-covered path, they turned left at the street, and left again as the cemetery came into view. A thin blanket of snow covered the graves, leaving little to the imagination—no tracks. Colbie closed her eyes as she had on previous occasions, tuning into the church. Her environment. "I'm not picking up on anything, at all . . ." She glanced at Brian. "Do you feel anything?"

"Nope—let's head to the back of the church . . ."

As they disappeared from street view, Brian noticed a

small door barely large enough to fit a grown man. "Hey! Check this out!" He let go of her hand, eager to pull on the small handle—as he did, the door creaked and opened slightly. "Holy crap! It's open!"

He held the door for Colbie, and both entered with a nagging feeling they shouldn't be there. "This is ten times creepier than the outside," Brian commented as he gently closed the door behind them.

The small foyer was the size of a postage stamp, its dank, musty smell unpleasant. "This place stinks . . ." Brian searched the wall for a switch, then realized turning on a light wasn't the most brilliant move. "Did you bring the flashlight?"

"Yep—the little one. It won't give us much light, but it will be better than nothing. Besides, we can't give away our being here . . ." Colbie took the small Maglite from her coat pocket, handing it to Brian. "I put in new batteries before we left . . ."

"Good girl!" He switched on the light, gently illuminating the tiny corridor into the main chapel, dust particles floating in the air as if searching for a new place to land. "This place can't accommodate more than fifty people," he observed as he strafed the beam of light, finally resting on a statue of Christ on the handmade altar. "I wonder if it's open for business every Sunday?"

"Exactly what I was thinking—I get the distinct feeling there's more going on here than simple community worship." Colbie glanced around the chapel, her eyes catching a glimmer of something close to a small baptismal font. "What's that?"

"What?"

"Over there—shine the light to the right . . ."

As the flashlight's beam reached the back wall, Colbie realized what caught her attention. "There's a door!" She inched closer, carefully taking in everything around her. "Let's see what's behind it . . ."

"Wait—let me go first . . ." Brian pulled her back, positioning himself in front of her.

For the first time, Colbie was okay with his taking the lead. "10-4 . . ."

The doorknob chilled his hand as it turned, and he pulled gently on the thick, handcrafted door. Shining the light into the dark, the thin beam revealed steep, wooden stairs leading to what seemed an inky pool of nothing. "I can't see shit—only steps."

"Can you see to the bottom?"

"Barely . . ."

"Well—let's check it out. I'll go first . . ."

Brian body checked her as she tried to move past him. "I don't think so . . ."

Shining the flashlight on the rickety steps, he tested the first one, gingerly placing his weight on one foot. Then, the other. "It seems okay . . ."

"I'm right behind you . . ."

As they descended, Colbie grabbed Brian's hand. "Oh, my God! Do you feel it?"

"Feel what?"

"Death—it lingers here . . ."

Brian stopped. "What? Death? What do you mean by that? Our deaths?"

Colbie closed her eyes. "No—the pastor. He died down here . . ."

"Shit . . ." His voice was barely a whisper.

Colbie bowed her head as if trying to invoke additional information. "Not just his—many deaths."

"Well, there is a cemetery . . ."

"That's not what I mean . . ." She raised her head, trying to focus on Brian in the dark. "Let's keep going . . ."

He nodded, shining the light before him. "Watch your step . . ."

To the right of the stairs was a small room with one chair positioned in its center and, as Colbie entered, her intuitive mind exploded with information. The pastor. His suicide. The depths of his unhappiness. "This is where it happened," she whispered, her voice taking on a reverence Brian hadn't previously heard.

"Where what happened?"

"The pastor's suicide—he stood on this chair, and wrapped a rope around that beam . . ." She pointed to the ceiling.

"So, it was suicide—I didn't think so . . ."

Colbie felt the disappointment in his voice. "It was—but he was driven to it . . ."

"By whom?"

Colbie concentrated on the chair and, in her mind's eye,

watching the suicide unfold, the number eight was at the forefront of her mind.

"Number eight on our list—he was here . . ."

"Hoffer? When?"

"During the suicide—he stood in the shadows, making certain the pastor did his part . . ."

Brian whistled softly. "You mean he forced the pastor to stand on the chair?"

"Yes—but the pastor didn't resist. It's like he wanted to go . . ."

"Maybe that's why I was so sure it was a suicide . . ."

Colbie nodded as she continued to watch the movie in her mind. "I'm sure of it . . ."

"What does Gregor Hoffer have to do with the pastor?"

"He was using the pastor for business—something the pastor couldn't get out of and he felt bound by deceit . . ."

Brian shook his head. "Why?"

Suddenly, Colbie's visions exploded with such force, she teetered, falling back on Brian. "Arms! This whole thing has to do with illegal weapons! That's why I saw the AK47s in my vision when we first started the case!" She opened her eyes, scanning the room. "Remember we thought about that, but, then, it didn't make sense!"

"I do remember—do you think Champagne was involved?"

"Good question—I'm not sure, but I think there's a good chance that's why he was taken out . . ."

They stood silently, thinking about the fragments of their case seemingly coming together. Finally, Brian spoke. "Let's get out of here—this is creepin' me out . . ."

****

"Have you ever heard of remote viewing?" Colbie skewered a piece of fruit, then paired it with a cube of cheese, popping both in her mouth at the same time.

"Maybe—I think I read something about it years ago. A military project, if I remember correctly . . ."

Colbie couldn't help smiling. Brian reading something about paranormal activities? *Maybe he was more engaged than I thought!* It was something she hadn't previously considered, and it felt good he was trying to learn about her abilities. She grinned at him as she chewed. "That's right! Back in the seventies and eighties, I think . . ."

"What about it?"

She took a sip of wine, then fiddled with another cube of cheese. "Well, I'm thinking of giving it a try . . ."

Brian took a sip of merlot, having no idea what Colbie meant. "What will that entail?"

"Intense concentration—even more than when I tune in to receive information about a case."

"I don't know, Colbie—after the bathtub episode, do you really think that's a good idea?"

Colbie felt a warm flush start from her neck. Even though Brian knew everything about her, it was still embarrassing he saw her at her weakest point. "What are you saying? Don't you think I'm capable?"

Brian eyed her, feeling a quick rush of anger. "Of course not—I know you can handle it. It just seems your visions regarding this case are already strong." He paused. "I worry about you. Your health . . ."

"Oh, for God's sake—do you think I'm losing my touch?"

Brian didn't answer.

Colbie stood, throwing her napkin on the table. "Well—do you?"

"I didn't say that . . ."

"But, you think it . . ." Colbie's eyes challenged him to tell the truth.

"Forget it, Colbie—you're not going to lure me into an argument!" He, too, threw his napkin, aiming it at the couch. Then, he grabbed his coat and headed for the door. "I'll be back later . . ."

Tears welled as Colbie watched him walk out. *Nothing's changed*, she thought. *I should have known better!"*

****

It must have been two in the morning before Brian quietly closed the door to their hotel room. He hated fighting with Colbie, but he disliked the way she tried to goad him into saying something he didn't mean. He fell for it for years and, when they rekindled their relationship, he silently vowed he wouldn't put up with it anymore.

All lights were off as he slipped off his shoes. It was weird she wasn't up—she often worked until the wee hours when on a case. "Colbie?"

Nothing.

She's probably still pissed, he thought as he hung up his coat. "Colbie? I'm back . . ."

Nothing.

That's weird . . . He walked quietly into their room. "Colbie? You awake?"

Nothing.

He flicked on the light—the bed hadn't been slept in. *Damn it, Colbie! Where are you?* As soon as that thought formed, he remembered the refrigerator—she would have left a note! He hurried to the tiny kitchen, fully expecting to see her illegible scrawl on a sticky note.

Nothing.

An eerie silence filled the room, and Brian didn't like it.

He didn't like it one bit . . .

****

"I know her—she's getting close. I can feel it . . ."

Nicole Remington didn't like the way things were turning out, and she questioned whether she made the right decision by bringing Colbie on board. The reality was there wasn't a bone in her body that cared about her brother's murder—the only thing he was good for was getting Colbie to Switzerland. Anything beyond that? She could care less. Now, however, she was beginning to think she acted hastily by hiring Colbie in the first place.

"If that's what you think, what are you going to do about it?" Harold's voice was impatient, knowing Nicole made a colossal mistake.

"That's just it—I don't know. I need to make sure I'm not backing myself into a corner. She's sly, and I'm beginning to think she's not telling me everything she knows . . ."

"You've always been impatient, Nicole—and, most of the time, it doesn't serve you well." Harold paused, wondering if it were worth his time to make her feel worse about herself. Probably not. "Well—like I asked—what are you going to do about it? If she's sniffing in your direction, you know what that means—it won't be long until she has you where she wants you. And, I suspect that's back in the slammer . . ."

Nicole knew he was right, and it was up to her to take care of matters within her control. "It's late—I'll figure it out, and let you know . . ."

"Act swiftly, Nicole—act swiftly . . ."

CHAPTER SEVENTEEN

———— ❖ ————

"Where the hell have you been?" As soon as Brian heard the door open, a sense of relief released all frustration and worry. "I've been worried sick!"

Colbie kicked off her shoes, not bothering to put them neatly by the door. "You're never going to believe it . . ."

"Try me . . ."

"First—I'm sorry I didn't get in touch with you, or leave a note. I knew you'd be worried—especially since we didn't part on the best of terms . . ."

Brian took her coat, and hung it in the closet. "Colbie— we may argue, but that doesn't mean I don't love you. And, it certainly doesn't mean I don't worry about you . . ."

"I know that—and, for what it's worth, I'm sorry." She

headed for the couch, glancing at the clock on the living room wall. "Did you happen to make coffee? I'm pooped . . ."

"I was just starting to brew it when you walked in the door. It'll be ready in a few minutes . . ."

"Thank God! Do we have anything to eat?" She punched the couch pillow to fit perfectly under her arm, putting her feet up on the coffee table. "I didn't want to take the time to stop at the corner market . . ."

Brian checked the fridge, reporting the bad news. "Nothing—I'll order room service. But, while I'm doing that, get your thoughts in order. I want to know everything . . ."

By the time he called, Colbie scrounged for a package of cashews she kept in her purse—they came in handy more than once. As she munched, she thought about where to begin—Brian wasn't going to be happy with her, of that she was certain.

"Chow will be here in about twenty minutes—I ordered your favorite . . ."

She looked at him, wondering how she could have argued with him. "Perfect—in the meantime, I'll polish these off." She playfully pitched a nut at him as he sat beside her.

He watched carefully as she tried to figure out how to tell him what she'd been up to. "So," she began, "I'm not sure where to begin . . ."

"Where did you go?"

"Well—right after you left, I got a phone call . . ."

"On the hotel phone, or your cell?"

"Cell—I'm still not certain who it was, but it sure sounded like Gregor Hoffer's secretary. The voice had a strong German accent . . ."

"Why would she call you? And, how did she get your private number?"

Colbie hesitated, finally taking the time to think it through. "I thought about that, and I figure it wasn't too difficult to lift it from her employer . . ."

"But, Hoffer never called you . . ."

"True—but Nicole did. My number wouldn't be that difficult to track down—who knows? Maybe she has friends in high places . . ."

"At this point, I guess it doesn't really matter—what did she say?"

Colbie shifted her legs, stretching them out full length on the coffee table. "It was brief—all she said was I should get to the church."

"The church? You went to the church? By yourself?"

Colbie swallowed hard—this was the part she knew was going to piss Brian off. "Yes—and, you'll never believe it . . ."

She was right—Brian was pissed. "What I can't believe is you went there by yourself in the middle of the night! What were you thinking?"

She fired off a serious look. "I may not have been thinking—but, the trip was worth it." She waited for his reaction, but got nothing but a look of expectation. "I saw Bachman, Hoffer, and Bruder. . ."

Brian was stunned! "At the church?"

"Yes—and, there were two other men . . ."

"But, why were they there? In the middle of the night, I mean . . ."

She paused, knowing she had his full attention. "They were digging two graves . . ."

Brian sat beside her, attempting to process what she just told him. "I'm not sure I get it . . . graves? For whom?"

"Well—that's the question, isn't it? I think they were there in the dead of night because they didn't want anyone to see them . . ."

"How do you know it was Bachman, Hoffer, and Bruder? And, who were the two other guys?"

"Oh, there was no mistaking them—as for the other two, I don't know. Toadies for whoever is pulling the strings, I guess . . ."

In the middle of contemplative silence, room service arrived, breaking the mood of the conversation. Brian tipped the young man generously, then wheeled the cart close to the couch and removed the two cloches. "Eggs Benedict, orange juice, and fresh strawberries—dig in!"

"You have no idea how hungry I am—I feel as if I haven't eaten for a week!"

By the time thirty minutes passed, both plates were empty, and they sipped on hazelnut lattes. He could tell she was beginning to relax, and he didn't want to push her—she would tell him everything in her own time.

She did. "It was pretty obvious, Bachman, Hoffer, and Bruder were supervising the men digging the graves. But, what really surprised me was what happened next . . ." A dramatic pause. "They extracted boxes from the graves . . ."

"Boxes? Of what?"

"I have no idea—from my vantage point, I couldn't make it out . . ."

Brian thought for a moment. "I think I know—weapons. AK47s . . ."

Colbie looked at him, stunned by his comment. "Weapons?"

"What else could it be? They need to have a way to move them, and it seems to me a tiny cemetery might be just the place . . ."

"You're right—it makes sense. Maybe that's why when I touched the headstones of a few of the graves, something didn't feel right—in fact, both of us commented on it more than once, if you remember . . ."

"I do—you said everything felt like a lie. And, that makes me wonder if there are bodies in any of the graves . . ."

Brian's statement left both of them with plenty to think about. "Still," Colbie commented, "why would they go to such lengths? Illegal weapons and gun running is commonplace, and they usually involve the seedier side of life—such as gangs."

"Precisely—I doubt they usually involve top banking executives . . ."

****

Reginald Champagne was hardly what one could call a ladies' man, although he fancied himself as such. Yes, he could be charming, but a good catch? Not really. A little too bipolar for some, and it was his changeling personalty that drove Nicole nuts as they were growing up. For someone who could be considered the laugh of the party, he often turned to a darker side to deal with his inner, true self—the truth was Nicole was the one who got the brunt of it most of the time. His parents, of course, considered him the golden child, refusing to acknowledge anything could be amiss with their boy. They turned the other way every time he did something considered socially unacceptable—especially when Camilla Parsons accused him of sexual assault.

"Our boy?" His mother's face was loaded with bullshit incredulity as the cops stood at their massive front door. "That can't possibly be . . ."

Ah—but it could! The lovely Camilla had proof, and she didn't hesitate to use it, thinking there could be a hefty payday in it for her and her family. "Ma'am—I know this comes as a shock, but we need to speak with you about Saturday night. May we come in?"

"I'm afraid not—I'm expected at a social gathering within the half hour . . ."

And, that's was it. Ever. No repercussions. No scolding. No demanding what he did to that poor girl. The accusations simply vanished, and it was a shock to the entire community when Camilla's father wound up floating in a lake just outside of town. "He must have been drinking," was the obvious reason and, for weeks, it was the talk of everyone who was anyone. But, gossip died down by the time Christmas rolled around, and all was forgotten.

And, forgiven.

Nicole considered the whole thing a bunch of crap—she knew her brother did it, and her parents did, too. Oh, yes—he had blood on his hands, and it seemed as if he didn't bother to wash it off. He carried on with life as charming as ever, and it was just another example of Reginald Champagne's machinations to get what he wanted from whomever happened to be available at the time. Anyone who got in the way? Well—there's always a price, isn't there?

Most of his conquests, however, didn't open their mouths for fear of the legendary Champagne wrath—doing so was Camilla's mistake. Everyone knew about it, but, still, they chose to remain mum—the thought of a lawsuit instigated by the Champagnes was enough to make anyone with a bank account of less than millions cower in unadulterated fear. It was no secret the Champagne empire would sue anyone if they felt they were wronged, and it was a state of affairs to make the stanchest of men cringe.

Then? College. Nicole went east, and Reginald turned his aspirations west—a situation that suited her just fine. They seldom saw one another except for holidays, and the rare family vacation—and, it wasn't until Nicole was in her final year that she introduced Harold to her brother.

A match made in heaven.

Instantly, the two young men bonded, often spending time sequestered in the Champagne library, hatching business schemes they hoped would work. In fact, they were so serious about their ventures, Reginald suggested Harold join him in the banking business, and Harold was all to eager to agree.

And, that was the beginning.

Reginald learned everything he could from his father and, when the old man finally croaked, he was confident he would make the Champagne name more important than ever before. By the time he was in his mid-thirties, he made Zurich his home, his connections spanning all social climes. As a young businessman, his father taught him he needed contacts in all areas of business, from the elite to the unelevated, and he made concessions to those he knew would help him in the future. "It's important to keep everyone happy," his father told him on his deathbed. "Run the business as if I were by your side . . ."

Of course, Reginald made his father's dying wish a reality, but only for a few weeks from the date of his funeral. After that, all bets were off—it was his business, and Reginald would run it as he saw fit.

By that time, Nicole's marriage to Harold was down the toilet, and Harold figured it was the perfect time to head for the Alps. From his arrival, Reginald included him in every facet of the banking game, including the unsavory types who surfaced occasionally, demanding something from someone. It was a part of the business Reginald didn't particularly like, but it was necessary—conducting deals in the dead of night became commonplace for the two men from the States, and ranking gang members were often those culminating their high-stakes games.

Dangerous, indeed.

So, it was one-by-one the two men increased their circle of colleagues, each new arrival bringing something to the table—and that's the way it was until Reginald's untimely demise.

The thing was Nicole knew about all of it from day one in spite of their taking care to keep her uninformed. That should be good for something, shouldn't it? Perhaps a little blackmail, at the least. She knew Harold was a Reginald Champagne sycophant, and she watched every move he made until he headed for the Alps. After that, she made it a point to stay in touch, knowing she would, one day, be a major player within their little group. She watched. Listened. Planned. And, it wasn't until after Harold split for the mountains, she made her first move.

She brought them business.

At first, she offered little black market deals to whet their appetites for something bigger and better, and it wasn't long until they began working in more illegal situations. Coupled with her successful real estate career in the states, she had a cozy little scheme going. Unfortunately, however, that's when things weren't adding up. Nicole suspected Harold was bilking her for a staggering amount of her proceeds, while Reginald was doing the same to Harold, Fischer, and Bachman. Including Hoffer, they were slow to catch on, but, eventually, they figured they weren't being paid according to their mutual agreements.

Something had to give.

An undercurrent of dissatisfaction continued until Reginald had enough. He called his band of men together, letting them know if things didn't change, he'd take his business elsewhere. "Everyone's expendable—keep that in mind," he said. His voice cold, cunning, and calculated, he made no excuses for his decision to disband if dissension continued. What everyone didn't count on was Reginald's ability to run a well-oiled organization—get rid of him, and things could go to shit in a heartbeat.

****

Colbie clicked off, setting her cell on the small table. "I was right—Tammy says Nicole's in Switzerland."

Brian pulled on his socks then stared at his shoes, deciding which pair to wear. "How does she know that?"

"Elementary sleuthing—she checked flight records. I think she knows someone who works at the airport . . ."

Brian pulled on his outdoor boots. "She has more friends in high places than I could ever have!"

Colbie laughed. "I guess that's what working at Optimum Security years ago did for her . . ."

Both busied themselves getting ready for their day, casually discussing their next move. When Colbie suggested they split up, Brian was having none of it. "I just don't think it's a good idea—you know as well as I do what Nicole Remington is capable of, and with her being in Zurich? I'm not too pleased to hear that . . ."

"Agreed—it's not the best situation. Nicole's being here kinks everything, and both of us need to be vigilant."

Brian couldn't help but think about Nicole Remington's kidnapping him, and who's to say she wouldn't try it again? He had yet to see her since she got out of the slammer, and he wasn't too thrilled about running into her in a foreign country. Who knows what contacts she had in Zurich? She certainly was in bed with Rifkin and Alvin before Colbie figured out their oil scam and, with her deviant personality, there wasn't a guarantee she wouldn't revert to the same behavior.

In fact, Brian would bet on it.

He sat on the bed, watching Colbie get dressed. He noticed stress creating a few new lines around her eyes and mouth, giving away her false confidence. "So—if we split up, where are you going today?"

She sat next to him. "I want to have a conversation with the Swiss authorities as I told Nicole I would. Since Reginald was in Zurich, they may be willing to part with information. If not, we need to do some digging to find out about his friends—those outside of his business connections."

"How do we do that? We don't have names—do we?"

"No—but I'm sure there are pictures of him at social gatherings on the Internet and in the Zurich papers— tabloids included . . ."

Within the hour, Colbie and Brian headed in different directions. He was to head to the library for research, and Colbie was off to see what she could learn from local police. Neither said anything as they split, leaving the hotel. They knew the drill, and both hoped they'd return that evening in pristine condition.

It wasn't a safe bet, though.

CHAPTER EIGHTEEN

Harold Remington was losing his patience. Nicole's being in Zurich certainly didn't help his mood, and the pastor's suicide was the last straw. Both served as beacons of his losing control, and it was time he regained it. "I don't care how you do it—get rid of her."

Gaspar Fischer shot him a steely stare. "Of course—but, are you certain you've given this enough thought?"

"What's that supposed to mean?"

"Just that Nicole's being here really doesn't impede what we're doing. She's a part of it, yes, but as long as you pay her the share she's due, I suspect you'll keep her happy."

Harold didn't say anything as he considered Fischer's reasoning. What Fischer didn't know was Nicole's purpose for being in Zurich was twofold—money, and Colbie Colleen.

"Maybe you're right . . ."

"Of course, you'll do what you think is right, but moving forward with your idea puts our operation at risk. I doubt it's worth it . . ."

"Agreed—that doesn't mean, however, we don't keep track of everything she does . . ."

Fischer stood, and buttoned his coat. "Shall I put our usual man on her?"

Harold nodded. "Tell him I want someone tailing her twenty-four seven . . ."

"Consider it done . . ." Gaspar Fischer pulled on his gloves, and headed for the door. "You will receive daily reports."

"You're damned right I will . . ."

****

Colbie arranged to meet with Lieutenant Simon Bollinger, senior detective investigating the Reginald Champagne murder, at ten o'clock. If she hoofed it, she could be there within thirty minutes—but, she felt like taking her time to think about everything that happened since their arrival in Switzerland. As she walked, she mentally cycled through the investigation, the most devastating discovery was her inability to recognize Nicole Remington's duplicity before she accepted the case. Did Brian resent her for it? She wasn't sure—nothing changed in his behavior, but that didn't mean he wasn't suppressing his true thoughts and feelings. In fact, chances were pretty good he was.

I don't blame him, she thought as she stood at the crosswalk across from the narrow condo building in the financial district. The more she thought about her self-perceived ineptitude, the more she realized her intuitive mind wasn't as strong as it used to be. That, too, was a crippling thought—for the last several months she retreated to her shadow world on a regular basis. There, she was safe, and no one knew she was depending on her other self to get her through the days. As a psych major coupled with her experience as a behavioral profiler, Colbie knew the dangers of such retreats—if she weren't careful, a pool of depression loomed, deeper than anything she previously encountered.

Within forty minutes, she stood at the polizei's reception desk, letting the young officer know she had an appointment—a few minutes later, she sat in front of Lieutenant Simon Bollinger. "Thank you for taking the time to meet with me." Sitting there, she was aware her greeting was the same as it always was. *Am I getting boring?*

"No problem, at all, Ms. Colleen—what can I do for you?"

"I'll get right to the point—it's my understanding you're heading up the Reginald Champagne investigation . . ." She waited for verbal or body language confirmation—nothing. "Do I understand correctly, Lieutenant?"

"I am. But, tell me, Ms. Colleen—why does Reginald Champagne interest you?"

It was time for the direct approach. "Because I was hired

by his sister to find out who killed him. Do you have any ideas?"

The lieutenant didn't answer immediately. It was never good form to give out information to someone he didn't know. However, before Colbie arrived, he did a full background check on her—and Brian. There was no doubt she was legit, and there was a possibility she could help him. The truth was they didn't have squat—only suspicions.

"Do you?"

Colbie got it. He wasn't going to divulge information until she told him about her investigation. "Nothing concrete. I'm hoping we can share . . ."

Lieutenant Bollinger agreed. "Perhaps we can help each other—what do you suspect? Or, perhaps, I should say 'whom' do you suspect?"

"How much time do you have?"

****

"Where are you now?"

"Outside police HQ . . ."

"What? What the hell are you doing there?" Nicole

Remington's impatience instantly ramped up to full-fledged anger.

"Because that's where she went . . ."

"You tailed her to police headquarters?" It took a moment for Nicole to realize exactly what he was telling her. "Don't go in—wait for her to come out, then pick up the tail again."

Jan Bachman grinned—exactly what he was going to do. However, he knew it made Nicole feel good when she was driving the bus—or, when she thought she was. "Roger that—I'll check in later."

****

Four hours passed before the update call, during which time Bachman surveilled his target from the station to a coffee shop, where she hung out for about an hour. She spent most of her time on the phone as she milked a latte—almost as if she were killing time and, from there, she began making the rounds of local gun shops.

That was the part he knew would interest Nicole.

He pressed three on speed dial.

"Took you long enough—what do you have?" Her voice was impatient, and it was clear she was growing weary of the cat and mouse game.

"After the police station, she went to a coffee shop for about an hour—she spent most of her time on the phone . . ."

"Then where?"

Bachman hesitated, knowing she wouldn't take the next part of his report well. "Gun shops . . ."

Nicole wasn't sure she heard him correctly. "Gun shops?"

"Yes—all of them within Zurich."

That information was enough to make her sit on the edge of her bed, her breath nearly gone. "After that?"

"The library—that's where I lost her."

Nicole Remington was silent as she processed every possible reason why Colbie was visiting gun shops. Clearly it had something to do with the case . . . *Is she onto me?*

"Nicole? You still there?"

Bachman's voice snapped her back to the current situation. "Yes—send a complete report immediately by courier."

"Anything else?"

"Yes—stand by to implement the plan—it's time . . ."

****

By six o'clock, Colbie and Brian were snug in their room. A light snow began to fall, making it a perfect night for staying in. Brian was already in his sweats, ready to take on the long night of reviewing notes he took at the library. "What do you want to order for dinner?" He knew the hotel menu by heart, as did Colbie.

"You know—I don't feel like a heavy meal. How about if I pop down the street to the bakery and cheese shop? That sounds really good to me . . ."

Brian put down the hotel menu. "Sounds good to me! I'll change . . ."

"Don't you dare! I'm still in my work clothes, so it makes sense I go—you're in charge of opening the wine." She grinned at him as she pulled on her boots, coat, and gloves. "I'll be back in a flash—do you have a cheese preference?"

Brian knew she was yanking his chain. "Nope—I'm sure you'll choose something perfect . . ."

With that, she was out the door.

Colbie's going by herself didn't sit well with Brian—but, ever since he'd known her, she refused to think she needed help from anyone. The way she viewed life, men and women were equal in most ways, and the ability to handle any situation was highest on her list. He learned years ago not to argue the fact and, a few times, it got him into trouble. Now? With Nicole in the picture, the danger level rose exponentially—something Colbie recognized, but she still refused to admit two were better than one. He thought she'd know that simply from her time on the force—but, being independent trumped safety most of the time.

He opened the wine, leaving the cork on the kitchenette counter. *By the time she gets back, it will be perfect . . .*

Except—it wasn't perfect.

By seven-thirty she still hadn't returned, and Brian's mind was teeming with possible reasons. Of course, he had to keep in mind she took off to the church without his knowing, and she returned hours later. *Everything's fine*, he told himself.

Everything's fine . . .

CHAPTER NINETEEN

By morning, she still wasn't back. There was no question something was desperately wrong, and Brian started making calls. "Tammy? It's Brian—have you heard from Colbie?"

Instantly, Tammy tensed, knowing Brian would never call her unless something were wrong. "Is Colbie missing?"

"I'm not sure—she left last night about six-fifteen to pick up cheese and bread from the bakery down the block."

"Holy shit, Brian! Tammy paused as she mentally calculated the time difference. "She's been gone fourteen hours?"

"I know—I figured I'd call you first. I guess your reaction means you haven't heard from her . . ."

Tammy sighed, and Brian could hear tears in her voice. "I haven't talked to her for a couple of days . . ."

"That's what I thought—if she calls, let me know immediately!"

He didn't wait for an answer.

As he thought of his next move, he noticed Colbie's messenger bag by the door—knowing her, she would have notes of everyone she saw or interviewed for at least a week. After rifling through it, there was only one set of notes they hadn't discussed—her interview with Lieutenant Simon Bollinger. *She must have taken his business card at the meeting because everything I need is right here . . .*

He dialed.

After three rings, a deep voice answered. "Bollinger . . ."

Brian swallowed hard. "Lieutenant Bollinger? My name is Brian Fitzpatrick . . ."

"What can I do for you, Mr. Fitzpatrick?"

"I'm calling about Colbie Colleen . . ."

Lieutenant Bollinger instantly recognized the name. "What about her?"

"She's missing."

Bollinger was quiet as he recalled his conversation with Colbie—she didn't seem the type to concoct something stupid. "When was the last time you saw her?"

"Around six-fifteen last night . . ."

"Maybe she was onto something—has she taken off before?"

Brian recalled when she visited the church in the middle of the night. "Yes—once."

But, by the time Brian explained everything, there was no doubt in Bollinger's mind something was, indeed, wrong. "What are you thinking? Since you're her partner, you must have some idea . . ."

"Not really—what I do know is it isn't good. Being gone so long isn't like Colbie . . ."

For the next half hour, Bollinger drilled Brian on the basics from did they have a fight to finally winding up with what he knew about the investigation she was conducting.

"I know everything about it—that's what scares me!" Brian paused, anger replacing unbridled concern. "If you want to know who killed Reginald Champagne, check out Harold and Nicole Remington!"

****

It wasn't long before Harold got wind of Colbie's being missing—and, it was with that revelation he recognized Nicole was a detriment to everything he built over the last decades. No longer could he put up with her poor judgment, and it was time he took matters into his own hands. So, under the guise of a business meeting, Harold—in his friendliest tone—requested Nicole's attendance. There was, of course, always the possibility of her becoming suspicious, but he phrased his invitation in such a way she couldn't refuse. "We need to discuss finances," he said. "I've been giving a lot of thought to our conversation, and, you're right—I haven't been aboveboard with you . . ."

Nicole, of course, knew his words were lies. "Really, Harold? Do you expect me to believe that?"

"It's up to you whether you believe it or not. However, if you're interested in discussing changes to our arrangement, you'll accept my invitation."

Nicole was silent as she considered whether she should attend the meeting. "Just the two of us?"

"Indeed—it's nobody's business, but ours." Harold paused, knowing she was about to take the bait. "You know I keep my business dealings close to the chest—this is no different . . ."

Again, silence. "What time—and, where?"

Harold smiled coyly—hook set. "How about this evening? I'll order dinner, and we can discuss our business at my office. Everyone will be gone, so there won't be anyone to bother us . . ."

"You're making it sound suspiciously like a date . . ."

Harold chuckled at her arrogance. "Would that be so terrible?"

She didn't answer his question. "Okay—the earliest I can do is six-thirty . . ."

"Excellent! I think what I'm going to propose will interest you . . ."

"It better, Harold. It better . . ."

****

Nicole had a penchant for being on time and, at precisely six-thirty, she buzzed Harold's office. Moments later, he appeared to escort her to upstairs. "You look lovely," he told her, checking her out from top to bottom. Another lie from the lips of Harold Remington—no matter how hard Nicole tried, prison took too much of a toll on her. Her face, he thought, was etched with deep lines around her mouth resembling jail cell bars—still, it didn't hurt to make her feel good about herself, especially since she wouldn't walk out of there feeling so great.

He kept his promise—dinner would be delivered promptly at six-forty five and, until then, small talk and drinks. Granted, it was only a fifteen-minute window, but he figured it was all he could stand. Knowing Nicole, she would press him to take care of business, and she really had no interest in social niceties.

That was an understatement.

"As much as I appreciate your efforts, Harold, I think we should discuss business without either of us having to play a game neither of us likes . . ."

He handed her a drink. "Oh, please, Nicole—is spending time with me that bad?"

She looked at him, assessing his sincerity. "It's not that—it's just I have . . . things to do." She took a sip, and smiled. "You know how it is . . ."

"I do . . ."

Just as he was about to introduce the tenets of what

he proposed as their new deal, the buzzer under his desk sounded. "Ah! There's our dinner now!"

It was a good thing he used the dinner service on many occasions—leaving Nicole alone in his office wasn't a good idea, so he directed the delivery man to meet him and, within a few minutes, filet mignon, roasted potatoes, and pan-seared broccolini were in front of them. "To better working relationships," he toasted, lifting his glass.

"And, just exactly what does that mean? It was my impression you weren't too fired up about giving me my fair share of the profits—so, if you're talking about a different monetary arrangement . . ." She paused. "I'm not interested."

"Even if your share is greater than it is now?"

She eyed him carefully. "Go on . . ."

"Don't get me wrong—I'm not turning over a new leaf. It's just I've been thinking about a few staff changes. And, if I go that route, it leaves more for me—and, you."

"What kind of changes?"

Harold casually sipped his wine, then placed the glass on the table. "I've been wondering about one or two of our colleagues—their loyalty. Although I don't have anything concrete to base it on, I get the feeling they have other irons in the fire . . ."

"So, if you do make a staff change, how does that affect me?"

He laughed, wondering if she were really that dense—he suspected she was. "It's pretty simple, Nicole—if they're out of the picture, that leaves more for us—you and me."

"And, how do you plan to do that without raising suspicion?"

Harold chuckled. "That's something you don't need to know—in fact, it's better if you don't."

Nicole fiddled with the fork on her plate. "There's just one thing—how can I trust you? It's not like you've been honest with me up until now."

"I know, I know. But, look at it this way—knowing what I just told you puts you in a good position. You'll have something on me—something to hold over my head."

Nicole sat back in her chair. "Perhaps—I'll have to think about it . . ."

"You do that—in the meantime, let's finish our meal! I'd hate for this lovely dessert to go to waste . . ."

By the time there was nothing but crumbs, Nicole was warming to the idea of Harold's proposition. She could always use the money, and he was right—she would have a strong position of blackmail at her disposal. "I'll think about it," she told again him.

"I suggest you don't wait too long—we have a deal coming to fruition soon and, if my plan is to work, I'll need to make arrangements."

She nodded.

"Speaking of plans," he commented, "how is your plan coming along?"

"Which plan is that?"

"You know—Colbie Colleen." If there were one thing he could count on, it was Nicole's endless need for revenge. He had to keep a close eye, however—one stupid move, and everything could be ruined.

"She's already taken care of . . ."

"What do you mean?"

"Just what I said—I had my men take care of the situation. Colbie Colleen is no longer a threat . . ."

He pushed his plate away, placing his napkin on the table. "Well—that changes things . . ."

"Changes things, how? Colbie doesn't have anything to do with us, or our business arrangements . . ."

"I'll be blunt, Nicole—it's not in my best interest to be in business with someone who acts irrationally. What did you do?"

"I gave her a taste of her own medicine, that's all— now we'll see how she gets herself out of . . . an untenable situation. Or, perhaps I should say *if* she gets out of an untenable situation . . ."

Harold's eyes narrowed to tiny slits. "I'll ask you again— what did you do with Colbie Colleen?"

Nicole hesitated, knowing she couldn't trust Harold as far as she could throw him. Still, she did have her position of power—the way she figured it, she was in charge. "Let's just say she's facing the same future as her boyfriend did several years ago . . ."

"You kidnapped her?" He didn't let on he already knew.

Silence.

"Am I right? You kidnapped her?"

Again silence.

His fist pounded the table. "What the hell have you done?" Harold's face flushed to an angry, crimson red.

"Relax—no one knows. In fact, her boyfriend is probably wondering right now why she hasn't come back to the hotel."

"How long ago?"

"Last night . . ."

In a flurry of anger, Harold swept his plate onto the floor, shards of glass and porcelain splintering in all directions. "How can you be so stupid? With her snooping around, and now she disappears? Did you stop to think that boyfriend of hers is going to go to the cops?"

Nicole didn't look at him. "I'm sorry . . ."

"You're sorry? You're sorry?" Harold's voice raised to a decibel level Nicole hadn't heard for years. He paced, his mind whirling with the possibilities of his underground operation going up in flames. "Go get her—get her, and take her back to the hotel! If you're lucky, he hasn't gone to the cops yet . . ."

"Are you out of your mind? If my men bring her back, she'll remember everything—well, maybe. It seemed prudent to keep her mind foggy—for obvious reasons."

Harold thought for a moment. "Good—have one of your men drug her heavily, then drop her off at the hotel. If it's late enough, no one will be paying attention, or they'll think she's drunk . . ."

"And, if she's drugged, how's she going to make it to her hotel room?"

"Trust me—the hotel won't want to compromise a patron's stay. Someone will help her to her room without creating a spectacle."

Harold saw no reason to tell her he already knew about

the kidnapping. As per his instructions, he had a tail on Nicole and Colbie twenty-four seven and, as soon as his investigator reported Colbie's leaving the hotel shortly after six the night before, his gut told him Nicole was up to no good. And, it didn't take him long to figure it out when Colbie didn't return. His man waited throughout the night, finally calling his boss at eight o'clock the following morning with the news.

Nicole leveled a steely glare at her ex-husband. "What difference does it make to you? You have nothing to do with it, and it's none of your stinkin' business! Besides, I said I'm sorry . . ."

Harold stood slowly, his temper a roiling boil, eyes boring down on her. "Listen to me—while you think you have the upper hand, you just played the wrong card. Now, I know what you did which puts me in a very interesting position, so listen carefully—get Colbie Colleen back in her room. I don't give a shit how you do it—just get her back there!"

"If I don't?"

"Don't be a fool, Nicole—I'll have eyes on you. If I hear that bitch isn't back in her room tonight . . ." Harold paused, and stood up straight. "Let's just say you don't know the level of my wrath. Now, get out! You have work to do . . ."

Harold thought he heard a resigned sigh. Nicole's shoulders slumped slightly as she stood to leave, and he quickly decided a soft word was in order even though it would be laced with insincerity.

"By the way—apology accepted."

****

The concierge ordered a bellhop to assist Ms. Colleen to her room shortly after one-thirty. "Avoid speaking to anyone," he advised, "and, if anyone speaks to you, pass off Ms. Colleen's condition to a little too much celebration . . ."

The bellhop nodded, placing his arm around Colbie's waist. "Do you want me to use the service elevator?"

The concierge thought for a moment. "Not a bad idea— yes, take her upstairs through the back . . ."

Colbie groaned slightly as the bellhop tried to hoist her into a workable position and, within five minutes, he stood in front of her hotel room door. He knocked, then waited.

No answer.

Carefully, he propped her against the wall as he slipped the key card into the lock. Without incident, he managed to get her seated in a chair, then left as quickly and quietly as he entered. As far as he knew, no one had a clue . . .

****

"It's done . . ."

As his man clicked off, Harold considered his next step.

It was clear Nicole was a loose cannon, and she couldn't be trusted. According to his investigator's report, she met with Gregor Hoffer and Jan Bachman and, an hour later? Colbie Collen was entering a hotel service elevator slapped up against a bellhop's hip.

It was at that moment Harold Remington made his decision. Earlier, he advised Fischer to get rid of Nicole—he didn't, however, specify a time frame. But, he knew Gaspar was efficient, and he fully expected to hear from him at any time. Now? With all the bullshit surrounding Colbie Colleen, he couldn't take any chances.

He fixed himself a scotch—rocks—then pressed four on speed dial. "Report . . ."

Gaspar Fischer switched his cell to the other ear. "You sound irritated, Harold. Is something amiss?"

"Don't give me your pompous bullshit, Gaspar—I'm not in the mood. We need to move up the operation . . ."

"Move it up? I thought you wanted me to wait until the most propitious time . . ."

"This is the most propitious time! I'm telling you to move it up—I want it done immediately!"

Fischer considered his options. "Understood . . ."

Harold rang off, anger simmering. *Sorry, Nicole—but you just became a liability . . .*

CHAPTER TWENTY

Exhausted, Brian returned to the hotel sometime close to dawn. Before heading to his room, he stopped at the front desk to check for messages—there were none, although he didn't really expect any. His heart dropped as he realized Colbie probably didn't have much time—statistics indicate the longer a person is missing, the less chance there is for a safe, healthy return—her time missing already rounded the twenty-four hour mark.

As the elevator silently ascended, he replayed the last twenty-four hours in his mind. Colbie's disappearance. His conversation with Bollinger. His countless questions to countless people, hoping someone may have seen her. Unfortunately, it was a three strikes, and you're out gig—he wasn't any closer to finding her than when he left.

The key card slipped effortlessly into the lock and, as he opened the door, he sensed something changed—something felt different. He closed the door quietly, and slipped off his shoes. "Colbie?" He waited several seconds before calling to her again. "Colbie?" Again, he waited.

"Brian . . ." Colbie's faint voice answered from down the hall.

"Colbie!" He rushed to the bedroom—there, she lay on the bed, her body curled in a loose fetal position. "My, God! Colbie!" Gently, he sat beside her, trying to assess her condition.

"Brian?"

"I'm here, Colbie—I'm here . . ."

She tried to speak, but her words slurred as if coming off a late-night bender. Other than that, however, she appeared to be alright—no discernible injuries as far as he could tell. He brushed a stray hair from her face, thinking she looked pale. "Can you tell me what happened? Where were you?"

Colbie slowly sat up. "I don't know . . ."

"You don't know what happened, or you don't know where you were . . ."

She tried focusing on him, his face barely more than a blob. "Both . . ."

Brian watched her closely. "I think we need to get you to a hospital . . ."

"No! Obviously, I'm drugged—all they'll do is keep an eye on me . . ." She offered a slightly lopsided smile. "And, I have you for that, don't I?"

"But, they can determine what kind of drug . . ."

"I know—but, does it really matter? The result will be the same . . . they'll keep an eye on me, then they'll send me home."

As much as Brian didn't like her refusal to go, he understood. When he tried to take his own life a few years back, he was in the hospital and it was much the same thing—except he decided to discharge himself. "Well . . . I don't like it, but I'll respect your decision."

"Wise man—now, help me into the living room, and I'll try to remember what happened."

"Nope—you're going to crawl into bed, and get some rest. You'll be much better equipped to deal with my questions once you have a few of hours of sleep under your belt . . ."

"But . . ."

"But, nothing . . ." He fluffed the pillows, and helped her get into her pajamas and, once under the covers, she was out.

Brian sat on the edge of the bed, watching for a few minutes, her right hand crooked toward her face. She lay perfectly still—a crescent sliver of early morning light stretched across the pillows, and he couldn't help but think she looked totally helpless.

It was then he vowed revenge.

****

A kid on a bike found her. It was kind of weird, too—he had no business being on that road and, only because he wanted to take a shortcut, did he see something sticking out from the winter-dead bushes. He wasn't sure what it was, but, as he inched closer, there was no mistake—a leg jutting into the air, bent at the knee, a shoe hanging precariously from a bluish foot—a high heel.

After a few expletives his mother didn't know he knew, he pedaled home without paying attention to anything but the road in front of him—and, after hearing his story, his mother called the police. Within thirty minutes, they cordoned off the area, and the coroner was on his way.

A cursory glance didn't tell them much—only that the leg belonged to well-dressed, fifty-something woman. Other than that? Nada. But, upon closer inspection, part of the woman's story started to make sense—two small holes at the base of her skull indicated there was nothing accidental about her death. Just like her brother, it appeared to be a professional hit.

Double-tapped.

****

"She was here when I got back early this morning . . ."

Bollinger listened to Brian's recount of Colbie's return to

the hotel. "Did she tell you why she was gone? Was it against her will?"

"She doesn't remember anything—it's pretty clear someone drugged her . . ."

"So—that most likely means someone snatched her the night she left the hotel. How is she now?"

"That's what I think—and, I'm willing to bet Colbie will think the same thing. She's doing better—still a little fuzzy, though . . ."

Bollinger thought for a moment. He had a lot on his plate, especially with the dead woman the kid found that morning. With everything he had to do, he didn't have time to look into Colbie's disappearance—if that's what it was. A tip came in regarding the Reginald Champagne case, and he couldn't spare men he didn't have. "Keep me posted . . ."

"Roger that . . ."

A couple of minutes later, Brian clicked off, leaving the lieutenant to his pile of work. He didn't doubt Colbie's disappearance was at the hands of someone else and, when he thought about it, the list of suspects was long—especially when he included numbers four, seven, and eight.

****

Lieutenant Bollinger waved in the young cop. "What do you have?"

"Prelims on the woman found earlier this morning . . ."

"Identity?"

"Remington—Nicole Remington." The young officer handed the report to his superior.

The stunned look on his superior's face didn't escape the officer as Bollinger flipped through the pages, scanning each line for pertinent information. "Thank you, that'll be all . . ."

Understanding the cue to scram, Gaines headed for the door, then turned. "That name sounds familiar . . ."

"It should—although not common knowledge, Nicole Remington was Reginald Champagne's sister . . ."

"That's it! I remember seeing her name in the paper right after Champagne's murder . . ."

Bollinger grinned at the young man. "You're going to make a fine detective one day, Gaines—a damned fine detective!"

Bollinger watched as Officer Gaines closed the door, then returned his attention to the Remington report. Although it was against precinct policy, he knew he should call Colbie—or, Brian.

****

"And—that's about it. I went out for cheese and bread and, the next thing I knew, someone stuffed me into a black van, and immediately blindfolded me . . ."

"Did you see his face?" Brian paused. "At least, I'm assuming it was a guy . . ."

"Good assumption—the guy was a hulk, but kept his face turned away from me. The one in the car wore a mask."

"Did you get a look at the car?"

"Yes, but not the license plate—black Mercedes van."

"What happened after they stuffed you?"

Colbie thought for a moment, still trying to clear the cobwebs from the previous night. "No one spoke, and I was trying to tune in on who was in the car with me . . ."

"Any luck?"

She nodded. "I think the man who crammed me into the Mercedes was Jan Bachman . . ."

"But, you didn't really see him . . ."

"True—but he felt familiar. And, the size of him is hard to miss . . ."

"Do you remember where they took you?"

Colbie shook her head. "No—but, it smelled damp."

"How long were you in the car?"

"Quite a while—but, I have the feeling they did some unnecessary driving to throw me off. You know I'd be taking mental notes of every turn—they knew it, too."

"Then what?"

Colbie looked at him, her eyes still a little dull. "I don't know—they kept me drugged . . ."

"Did they feed you?"

"Some—but, it was nothing but junk. I guess they didn't feel like preparing a home-cooked meal . . ."

"How did you wind up here?"

"It was hard to keep track of time because of the blindfold, but I think it was in the middle of the night—the same big guy came in, zip-tied my hands, and led me to a car. The next thing I know, I was in the hotel room, sitting on a chair. How I wound up on the bed, I don't know—sheer determination, I guess . . ."

Just as Brian was about to ask another question, Colbie's cell vibrated.

Bollinger.

****

Colbie clicked off, a stunned expression on her face. "You're never going to believe this . . ."

Brian looked up from the notes he took about Colbie's kidnapping, although there weren't many. "What that?"

"Nicole is dead . . ."

"What? You're kidding me! Who was that on the phone?"

"Bollinger—a kid found her body early this morning out on a country road. From what Bollinger told me, she died the same way her brother did . . ."

"Execution style?"

Colbie nodded.

"Holy shit!" He paused. "Does this mean we don't get paid?"

"Brian!"

"Oh, c'mon! You can't blame me, can you? And, you have to admit chances are good she was involved in your kidnapping . . ."

Colbie was quiet for a moment. "You're probably right about that—and, obviously, someone wanted Nicole out of the way. The question is why . . ."

"And, who . . ."

****

Bollinger held his identification right in front of the receptionist's face so there was no mistaking he was on official business. Since learning of Nicole's death, the investigation into Reginald Champagne's death amped up tenfold and, because he couldn't see Colbie until later that afternoon, he decided a little chat with Harold would be a good way to pass the time.

The first time they met was only a few days after Reginald turned up in the drink, and Bollinger decided in the first thirty seconds he didn't like the looks of him. *An arrogant bastard*, he thought, and he knew Remington had something to do with Champagne's murder—he just didn't know what.

After the go-ahead from the receptionist, Bollinger headed for the top floor, relishing the thought of watching the look on Remington's face when telling him about Nicole's unfortunate demise—that's if he didn't know about it already. And, that was the thing—it really could go either way because an ex-husband may not show emotion. After all, they were divorced, and rumor had it Harold enjoyed the high life. Literally. But, after reviewing everything he had on Harold Remington, he realized it wasn't much—the man was a master of the underground.

The elevator doors opened silently, and Bollinger stood at heavy glass doors leading to Remington's office. A young woman sat at her desk, eyes trained on the door— obviously, anyone making a trip to the penthouse office suite announced their arrival before they left the ground floor, and her expectant look allowed the lieutenant little time to assess Harold's surroundings.

Slowly, the door opened silently, offering him the opportunity to enter. "May I help you?" Monique's voice was soft and silky.

Before answering her question, Bollinger showed her his identification. "Harold Remington, please . . ."

"I'm afraid Mr. Remington . . ."

"Look—Monique—I know he's in. How about if we try this again? I need to see Harold Remington—now!"

"Yes, Sir—I'll buzz him . . ."

Within a minute, Harold Remington opened his office door. "Monique—take a break." Then he focused his attention on Lieutenant Bollinger. "Lieutenant! What brings you to the financial district?" He stepped aside with a sweeping gesture, inviting Bollinger into his office. "Please—have a seat . . ."

The lieutenant took his time getting situated, watching Remington's every move as he settled in a the chair behind his desk. A cursory glance of the office indicated a minimalist decorating style, and he couldn't help wondering if that represented his life, as well. "Mr. Remington—I'm hoping you can help me . . ."

"Help you? With what?"

Bollinger again took his time. "A murder . . ." He watched Harold's face carefully—not a flicker of anything.

"A murder?" Harold leaned back in his chair. "Are you talking about Reginald?"

"No—at least not right now."

Harold shifted slightly. "Then, who?"

"Your ex-wife—Nicole Remington . . ."

Harold played his part to perfection. He stared at the lieutenant for a moment, then at his desk. "What?" He paused for a moment of dramatic dismay. "How? When?"

"We won't know until the official coroner's report, but we suspect she died within the last twenty-four hours . . ."

Harold kept staring at his desk. "How?" He was well

aware the lieutenant hadn't answered his question.

"From first appearances, she was shot twice at the base of her skull . . ."

Harold's head snapped up. "Are you saying she was . . ."

"Murdered? Yes—that's exactly what I'm saying."

Of course, Harold knew why Bollinger was sitting in his office. "What do you need from me," he asked as he took off his glasses, holding them lightly in his fingertips. "How can I help?"

Bollinger studied him and, for the first time in many years, he couldn't get a good read. "Well, to start—where were you for the last twenty-four hours?"

"Me?" He thought for a moment, as if recalling his schedule. "I was here until about nine-thirty, as usual—then I went home. That's it . . ."

For the next fifteen minutes, Bollinger grilled Harold, but there was nothing suspicious to tip him off about Nicole's ex being involved. Yet, he didn't believe it. As sure as he sat across from Harold Remington, he knew Remington had a hand in Nicole's death. But, could he prove it?

Not yet.

CHAPTER TWENTY-ONE

B y the time Bollinger rapped on Colbie's hotel door, she was back to normal. The drug took it's time wearing off, but a cool shower finally helped her regain her faculties—by the time the lieutenant arrived, she recalled everything. Unfortunately, it wasn't much. "I know," she said, "but, when they stuffed me in the van, I had little time to pay attention to anything . . ."

Bollinger turned off the recorder between them on the small dining table. "Chances are good you won't remember much more—designer drugs these days are sophisticated and for specific results. I imagine they drugged you with something that will prevent you from remembering—ever."

Colbie thought about that for a minute, uncomfortable with the thought she may never regain those memories. "So—what did you learn about Nicole's murder? As you know, she was my client, but my gut tells me she had her fingers in more than one pie." She paused. "As much as I hate to admit it, she duped me—and, it became clear her main plan was to get me out of the picture . . ."

"The question is," Bollinger commented, "why did someone want her dead?"

Colbie thought for a few seconds before answering. "Have you looked into Harold Remington in depth? He's a charming man, but he has a black streak running through him . . ." She paused again. "Have you looked into his heading up a possible gun running operation?"

The lieutenant glanced at Brian, then back at Colbie. "Gun running? Why do you think he's involved in something like that?"

Colbie swallowed, and looked at Brian who nodded his agreement it was time to level with the lieutenant about her intuitive capabilities. "Because . . . I have certain abilities allowing me to see inside a person's motives or actions . . ."

Bollinger looked confused. "I'm not sure what you mean. Are you telling me you're psychic?"

"In a word—yes. It serves me well in my cases . . ."

"In fact," Brian interjected, "it's her abilities that put her on the map in the profiler world. She's accurate as hell . . ."

It's not that far-fetched, the lieutenant thought as he processed Colbie's admission. He worked with a psychic in his early days as a detective, and he found the experience interesting as well as enlightening. "Okay—so, tell me what you think about this case. Did you see or feel something that leads you in the direction of Harold Remington's heading up an illegal arms operation?"

Colbie nodded. "At the very beginning—I also saw a small church." She looked Bollinger in the eye. "We found the church outside of Zurich, but I haven't been able to hone in on the weapons . . ."

"What about the church—what's going on with that?"

She glanced at Brian, knowing they were in the church illegally. "We managed to get into the church, and there's a room downstairs that triggered all of my senses." She hesitated, thinking of what she and Brian saw. "Do you remember the pastor who committed suicide a little while back?"

Bollinger nodded.

"Well, that's where it happened. And, I now know he was forced into it—although, to be fair, the pastor was up to his neck in something he didn't understand. I get the feeling he was a middle man of some sort . . ."

"What makes you think that?"

"Because, when we were there, I had a vision, and I saw another man—whom I now believe to be Gregor Hoffer— pulling the strings . . ."

"Gregor Hoffer? Now, there's a familiar name . . ."

"You'll probably recognize a few more names I think are instrumental in the underground operation . . ." Colbie paused as Bollinger flipped to another page in his notebook. "Gaspar Fischer and Jan Bachman—and, of course, you already know about Harold Remington . . ."

Bollinger glanced at Brian, then refocused on Colbie. "Let me make sure I understand—are you telling me Gaspar Fischer, Gregor Hoffer, Jan Bachman, and Harold Remington are running illegal arms?

Colbie smiled at the lieutenant. "Yep—in fact, I'm sure of it . . ."

"Then what did Nicole Remington have to do with it?"

"Oh, she knew plenty—I believe she and Harold were in cahoots because of the money . . ."

Bollinger thought for a moment. "In cahoots and divorced? I'm not sure that makes much sense . . ."

"Believe me—it makes perfect sense. Nicole was a woman filled with hate and revenge, and I think she spearheaded my kidnapping based on that need to get back at me . . ."

"Revenge for what?"

For the next hour Colbie and Brian filled the lieutenant in on Brian's kidnapping, the oil scam, and Nicole's time in the slammer. She told him about Nicole's hiring her under the guise of finding out who killed her brother, as well as her veiled relationship with Harold. "Oh, they hated each other's guts," she told him. "But, money trumps emotional turmoil and, somehow, they found a way to work together."

Bollinger glanced at Brian. "That's why you said at the end of your call to look into Harold and Nicole Remington—then, it didn't make much sense, but now? I think you're right—this is the major break we need . . ."

****

"Get your ass over here! And, bring Hoffer and Bachman with you . . ."

Gaspar Fischer listened intently, irritation simmering at his boss's direct order. "I'm not certain . . ."

"Apparently, you didn't hear me—you have thirty minutes . . ." With that, Harold Remington clicked off, certain they would be there within the half hour—it would be foolish to do otherwise.

The reason for the meeting? His dissatisfaction with Fischer's sloppiness—finding and identifying Nicole within twenty-four hours? Not what he expected from his right-hand man—which is why he was becoming more certain Fischer had another gig. During the last several weeks, he maintained a low profile, and doing so was out of the norm. It was no secret wherever Gaspar chose to go, there was a little flair—even if it were only the simple task of taking off his gloves. Heads turned as he walked by, the fragrance of money wafting to anyone recognizing the scent of the buck. Now? He reminded Remington of a startled cockroach scurrying into a dark, dank corner.

Even so, dissatisfaction with Fischer wasn't the only thing he needed to address—the manner of Nicole's death topped his agenda. Harold no longer trusted the men whom he held close, and he had to be certain he wasn't being compromised by a trio of fools. Were Hoffer, and Bachman drifting away from him, too? Was there a possibility they could throw him under the bus?

The more Harold Remington thought about it, the more he knew it was time to revamp his little organization.

Time to reel in a favor . . .

****

"But, I can feel it . . ." Colbie leaned against the railing in the elevator, trying to figure out who was really pulling the strings surrounding Nicole's murder.

"I don't really care what you feel—after the last couple of days, I'm not going to let you out of my sight . . ." Brian waited until the door closed before continuing. "I don't care if it does slow us down. Besides, with Nicole taking a permanent powder, we really don't have a client, anymore . . ."

"True—but . . . we were hired to find out who killed Reginald Champagne, and he we haven't done that yet."

"Well, I gotta tell you, I'm not too wild about working for free . . . we can be here for months and, after all that's happened, I'm just as happy to head back to the States."

"I know—and I don't blame you. You've handled this whole thing better than I, and I don't have any right to suggest staying to see the case to the end . . ."

"Oh, please—granted, it's been a little tough. But, I'm not a quitter. This has to be your decision—can you bill Nicole's estate for your fees?"

"Maybe—I'll ask Tammy to check. I'm pretty sure I can."

Brian held the elevator door as Colbie eased in front of him, stepping into the lobby. "Find out. How about this—if you can bill for fees, we stay. If not, we hit the road . . . deal?"

"Deal . . ."

****

Harold sat at his desk, staring at the three men in front of him. Bachman reminded him of Shrek, his hulking body barely fitting in the modern, sparse-looking chair. Hoffer didn't look any less uncomfortable, and he surreptitiously glanced at Gaspar Fischer, arching his right eyebrow.

Harold continued to stare.

Fischer arranged his gloves on his lap, smoothing them with his palm as he always did. "So, Harold—why did you summon us so abruptly? I gather you're displeased?" Fischer had a penchant for understatement, a trait rankling Remington since they met.

"You might say that . . ."

Gaspar met his boss's gaze. "Then spit it out, Harold—what has your knickers in a wad?"

And, there it was—what Remington suspected for weeks. Gaspar Fischer no longer respected him, and his insolent question proved it.

Harold ignored the question. "I have concerns," he began, "about the quality of your work . . ."

Fischer took the lead as spokesman. "Our work?"

"For God's sake, Gaspar—wipe off the incredulous look. You know exactly what I'm talking about . . ."

"I'm afraid I don't . . ."

"Bullshit! Since when have you taken care of business

for me, and the results are discovered in less than twenty-four hours?" Harold laced his voice with controlled anger. "Are you out of your mind?"

"Really, Harold—everything we did . . ."

"Was sloppy and inefficient! Nothing like making it easy for the authorities, not to mention Colbie Colleen . . ."

Fischer sat silently for a moment—he hadn't considered Colbie Colleen sticking her nose into things. But, it made sense—he knew for a long time Nicole hired the investigator, but it didn't occur to him she would stay on the case after Nicole's unfortunate demise. "Why does she have anything to do with us? She can't prove a thing . . ."

Remington shifted in his chair. "Have you read her bio? She doesn't give up . . ."

Again, Fischer smoothed his gloves. "I think you're grasping at straws, Harold . . ."

Harold stood, his tall frame looming over his desk. "I don't give a shit what you think!" He paused. "Which brings me to the reason for this meeting. It occurs to me I can no longer trust any of you to carry out my orders professionally, and to the best of your ability. My bitter ex-wife's death proves that . . . so, it's in my best interest to sever professional ties. As of this moment, I am terminating our association. That said, if you choose to not accept my decision gracefully, I suggest you watch your backs. Now—get out!"

As the verbal venom settled, Harold couldn't help thinking about the time a few months earlier when he tried to get rid of Fischer and Hoffer in Gruyères. It was a good idea then, and it was a good idea now.

Finally, he sat, small beads of sweat tracing the side of his temple.

"Don't you think you're being a bit rash?" Fischer refused to show disdain for Harold, but he could let him know—via innuendo, of course—he wasn't wild about the decision. After all, he didn't truly work for Remington—their working together outside of normal business hours was agreed upon by mutual consent. Remington, however, seemed to believe he was running the show. And, he was—their operation was his baby, no matter what Fischer, Bachman, and Hoffer thought.

"Not at all—now, as I said—get out!"

The three men rose silently, heading for the door. Fischer ceremoniously buttoned his coat, turning to look at Remington before leaving. "You're making a mistake," he warned, pulling on his gloves.

"A mistake? I don't think so, Gaspar . . . you'll receive final payment for our last transaction by the end of the day."

"You know this isn't about money . . ."

"Then what is it about, Gaspar?"

Fischer allowed an amused grin. "Power, Harold—it's always about power . . ."

****

Flanked by two body guards, the leader dismounted, then approached. No handshake. No greeting. Clearly, he had little time to waste as he stood in front of Harold Remington, arms crossed—there was no mistaking what he did for a living. Tattoos streaked up his arms and neck, a single teardrop inked permanently under his left eye.

He waited.

Remington nodded. "I'll be brief. Over the years, we've been straight with each other, right?"

The human brick wall nodded, glancing at his two men.

"I'm sure you'll agree," Remington continued, "we've done a few favors for each other along the way . . ."

Another nod.

"That's why you're here—I need a favor . . ."

A slight snort. "I figured that—who, and when?"

A slight smile played on Remington's lips. If everything went according to plan, there was little to prevent him from cashing in. "As soon as possible . . ."

Twenty minutes later, three Harley's roared from the deep recesses of the parking garage, leaving Remington to his thoughts.

It was done.

****

"I can? Well, that means you'll be holding down the fort for a while longer . . ."

"No problem—I'm responding to all prospective client calls immediately, and word is out you're out of the country on a case."

"Good—keep in touch, and I'll call in a few days. The way everything is changing, who knows what will happen?"

Tammy chuckled. "No kidding!" She paused before asking the question bugging her since she found out about Nicole's death. "Who did it? Any idea?"

Colbie accepted a cup of hot chocolate as Brian passed her on his way to the couch. "I have an idea, but I don't have proof. I haven't even discussed my thoughts with Brian . . ."

"Well, maybe you should. How's he handling everything? I mean, it's gotta be hard on him dealing with Nicole Remington, dead or alive . . ."

"I'm sure it is, but he says he's fine . . ."

After five minutes of discussing office needs, Colbie rang off, thinking about Tammy's question. *Is he really okay,* she wondered. Brian was good a hiding his feelings, and she felt she needed to constantly observe to get a handle on things. Even so, she had to trust him when she couldn't trust herself."

And, that was happening a lot more lately.

CHAPTER TWENTY-TWO

Three men entered the banker's office, each buried under the weight of his own thoughts. Theirs was a precarious position, and lying low might be the best answer, at least for Bachman and Hoffer—Fischer, however, was a different story. As much as he tried, anger leached from every pore, his face set with ideas for revenge. No— even though Gaspar Fischer wasn't really 'fired,' he wasn't taking a substantial decrease in his income lightly.

There would be hell to pay . . .

"Close the door . . ." A deep voice from behind a massive desk barked his order, casting aside any semblance of professionalism. "Sit down . . ."

Fischer glanced at his colleagues, his expression confirming he had first choice of chairs in front of the desk.

Bachman and Hoffer deferred and, within moments, each sat silently.

"Your call, Gaspar, sounded urgent . . ."

Gaspar Fischer hesitated, knowing if he chose his current course, pawns would fall. Kings, too. "It appears we have a considerable problem . . ."

"Regarding?"

"Remington. Harold Remington . . ."

Christoph Anderegg leveled a steely stare at Fischer, waiting for Gaspar to spit it out. "Well?"

"He terminated our professional association . . ."

Anderegg sat silently, thinking the three men sitting across from him must have done something stupid in order to piss off Remington to the point of canning their sorry asses. "Because?"

Bachman and Hoffer shifted in their chairs, eyes on Fischer. "Because of that bitch ex-wife of his . . ." Fischer smoothed his gloves with his right palm.

Twenty minutes later, the room was silent. *Perhaps Remington was right—maybe they were sloppy with Nicole's disposal . . .* That, however, didn't make any difference—he anticipated Remington's power grab. One thing Anderegg abhorred was a power-hungry minion—and, that's exactly what he thought of Harold Remington. More than once he overlooked Remington's poor decisions when it came to the operation, and his behavior was beginning to get on his nerves. All it would take was for someone to slip up, and everything he worked for would be ruined. But, if he chose to deal with matters himself, there was always the risk of discovery. Not only that, he had that upstart of an investigator to deal with—he had a feeling Colbie Colleen could—and, most likely, would—become a problem.

That was the last thing he needed.

By the time Fischer, Bachman, and Hoffer stepped into the icy sunshine of a late winter's day, their orders were already in motion. Gaspar Fischer pulled on his gloves, eyeing his colleagues. "I trust you're clear?"

Both men nodded.

Without word, the three men parted, each going his separate way, thinking about the next twenty-four hours. But, there was already a chink in the plan—one which never occurred to Gaspar Fischer. Jan Bachman had a thing for Nicole Remington, and his admiration of her was enough to entertain the idea of revenge. "Whatever you need," he once told her, "and I'll have your back. You can count on it . . ."

And, that's just what he intended to do.

****

"So—that's the deal. As far as Tammy could figure out, she can bill Nicole's estate for fees . . ."

"Then—that means we're staying. Right?"

"Do you want to?" Colbie watched Brian's response, looking for any indication he was going to hand her a line of bull. She appreciated his willingness to do anything for her, but it was important he didn't overlook his own needs.

He sat behind the wheel of their rental car, thinking about years past—years forward, as well. "I have to admit, I see your point—we were hired to achieve a certain result. Bailing now seems stupid . . ."

Colbie nodded. "I can't help but feel the same. You know I don't like to leave things unresolved—and, I have a feeling we're about to discover something that's been keeping us from knowing the truth."

"Such as?"

"Well—let's look at Harold Remington. What do we know about him?"

"He's a ladies' man—and, he'll stoop to anything to get his way . . ."

"True—plus, money is his main motivation."

Within the half hour, between the two of them, they managed to build a solid profile of Nicole's ex-husband. "The final question we have to answer," Colbie observed, "is do we think Harold Remington killed Reginald Champagne?"

Brian took his time answering. There was a part of him thinking Harold was the trigger man—but there was something about that theory not making sense. "To be honest—I don't think so . . ." He glanced at Colbie. "What do you think?"

Again, Colbie agreed. "Whatever the depth of the arms operation, Harold's involved in it somehow. I just don't think he's the one who murdered Champagne. Besides, doesn't Harold strike you as the type of person who doesn't want to get his hands dirty?" She paused, closing her eyes. "I get the feeling Harold Remington likes being the boss—he'd never stoop to such treachery when he could have someone else do it."

Brian cranked up the defrost—condensation on the windshield was quickly turning to ice as the two investigators considered how to proceed. "Here's my question—who, as you say, sits on top of the pyramid? Is it Remington?"

"Excellent question—or, is there someone we haven't considered?"

And, that was the thing. Was there someone they hadn't considered? Someone who pulled the strings for professional and personal monetary gain? Perhaps.

It was something to think about . . .

****

Slicing rain stung Bachman's face as he stood at the back of the tiny cemetery, shovel in hand, mulling over his best options. Headstones tilted to the right or left, the abuse of decades scarring their faces, leaving no clue there wasn't a body underneath the fertile ground.

He began to dig.

As far as Bachman saw it, there wasn't any reason to drag things out when Fischer arrived. If he showed up with Hoffer, things might get a little sticky—he sure as hell didn't put it past Fischer to bring along a body guard. But, if he showed up solo, his plan was a go.

Bachman turned as headlights flicked off, the car parking in front of the church. Within moments, Gaspar Fisher stood before him. "Okay—I'm here. What's so important we couldn't discuss it in Zurich?"

"Just this . . ." Bachman raised the silenced pistol and fired once, relishing the surprise on Fischer's face.

Fischer dropped where he stood, his head landing perilously close to the grave's marker. Without hesitation, Bachman sealed the deal with one more shot to the back of the neck.

****

"This case has turned into a real mess . . ." Colbie shoved her chair back, disgusted. "I've been thinking of everything that's happened since we arrived in Zurich . . ."

"And?"

"We don't have crap! I feel as if we're starting at square

one . . ."

Brian closed his laptop, giving her his full attention. "I disagree—when we first got here, we didn't know about the numbers four, seven, and eight. We didn't know Nicole Remington was as much as a snake in the grass as I thought."

"Yes, but that knowledge hasn't gotten us anywhere, and we don't have a main suspect for who killed Reginald Champagne . . ."

"You're right about that—we finally decided Harold Remington didn't pull the trigger. But, that doesn't mean his hands are clean—he may have had someone do it for him."

Colbie tossed her pen on the table, considering Brian's idea. "Who?"

"I'm guessing it's one of the people on Nicole's list—the one you went over with Anderegg."

"Fischer, Bachman, or Hoffer . . ."

"Right. Of those three, who do you think is most likely to murder someone, Mafia style?"

Colbie pulled her knees up to her chest, then wrapped her arms around her legs. "Of those three, I think I'd have to choose Jan Bachman . . ."

"Why?"

"Because he looks like a thug—his size immediately intimidates . . ."

"That's what I think—he looks like the hired-gun type."

"So—the next question is who would hire him? Who would keep someone like that on his payroll?"

Colbie thought for a minute. "Either Gaspar Fischer or Harold Remington . . ."

"Bingo! And I'll bet my last dollar it's Remington . . ."

****

It was nearly dawn by the time Jan Bachman took the long way around to his car. The whole thing took longer than he thought—top layers of dirt were frozen, slowing his progress. But, by the time he patted the shoveled earth down, then added weather-worn sod, the grave looked as if it had been there, undisturbed, for years. *Not bad*, he thought, as he admired his work. He had to admit, Gaspar's idea was brilliant . . .

By the time he arrived back in Zurich, there was only enough time to shower, dress, and head out to meet Hoffer.

Time for a new plan.

****

Three weeks passed, no one the wiser about anything. Colbie and Brian worked relentlessly to determine Reginald's killer, but they didn't come up with much. "I decided to interview everyone on the list again," she mentioned as they climbed into their car. She adjusted her coat, making sure it was smooth against the seat. "I haven't been able to secure an appointment time with Gaspar Fischer, or Jan Bachman."

Brian pressed the ignition, then checked the instrument panel to adjust the defrost and heat—Colbie was the last one to drive it, and she liked the heat blasting directly on her. Him? Not so much. "Out of town?"

"That's what their secretaries say, but I don't believe it. What do you say to a little surveillance?"

"Cool with me!"

"Good—let's start with Fischer's office. He may show up during the night, thinking no one will be paying attention."

"What about that restaurant? The one where you first met him?"

Colbie nodded. "Good idea—in fact, let's start there. If he goes for something to eat, I'll bet it will be right before the restaurant closes—fewer people to take note."

"Tonight?"

"Tonight . . ."

****

Two men stood over what looked like—from a distance—a pile of dirt. It wasn't until they approached, did 'body' come into the conversation—and, as soon as it did, they were on the horn to the authorities. It wasn't long until the area was cordoned off, several police officers on the hunt for clues. And, before the sun set, the unfortunate victim of foul play—bullet holes in his skull were the first clue—was on his way to the morgue.

Of course, it couldn't have been simple for authorities. At least ten officers scoured the crime scene for anything giving them an idea about the man's identity—but, there was nothing. No wallet. No I.D. No jewelry.

As darkness closed in, they knew little.

****

By the time the body reached its destination, Lieutenant Bollinger was already on his way. "I'll be there in ten . . ." he advised the coroner as he hung up. Normally, he wasn't the first to arrive to a pending autopsy—this time, however, he had a gut feeling something was different about the vic. Why, he didn't know—but, his thought to get in touch with

Colbie Colleen, turned out to be a good one.

Nearly done with their restaurant surveillance, Bollinger's call came just at the right time. Within the hour, Colbie, Brian, Lieutenant Bollinger, and the coroner stared at the body on the gurney, its toetag blank. Stunned, Colbie was the first to speak. "That's Gregor Hoffer . . ." She turned to Brian, her eyes wide. "Don't you recognize him?"

"Now I do!"

"How do you know that?" Lieutenant Bollinger glanced at them, then at the coroner.

"Because I recognize him from our investigation! Remember my telling you about the list of potential interviews Nicole Remington gave us? And, what Christoph Anderegg whispered when I was leaving his office?"

Lieutenant Bollinger struggled to recall the conversation. "To be honest, not really . . ."

Colbie turned to him, eyes flashing with excitement. "He told me to look at the numbers four, seven, and eight— Gregor Hoffer was number eight on the list!"

"What's the significance of the numbers?"

Colbie turned her attention back to Hoffer lying as stiff as a two by four in front of her. "I don't know—but, you know what's weird? I've been trying to get in touch with Gaspar Fischer for nearly a month . . ."

"What does that have to do with this guy?" The coroner focused directly on Colbie.

"Gaspar Fischer was number four on our list." Colbie paused, thinking about the list Nicole gave her. "It seems to me someone is picking off executives at an alarming rate.

The only one left is number seven—Jan Bachman.."

"You think he's culling the herd?"

Colbie shook her head. "I'm not sure—but, I'm going to get in touch with him for another interview . . ."

Within the half hour, Bollinger, Brian, and Colbie stood in front of the morgue, plotting their next move. "Everything will rest on my second interview with Bachman—if I can get ahold of him. If not, I'll have to figure out something else . . ."

CHAPTER TWENTY-THREE

" Ms. Colleen—how nice to see you again!" Jan Bachman extended his hand for a dead fish handshake, a social trait Colbie found particularly repugnant.

"Thank you for seeing me on such short notice . . ."

"Nonsense! It's no problem, at all . . ." He guided her to a chair beside a small table as he sat on the opposite side. "Now—what can I do for you?"

Enough of the niceties. "When we first met several months ago, I told you I'm investigating the murder of Reginald Champagne—his sister, Nicole, hired me." She waited.

"I recall . . ." *What does that have to do with me*, he wondered as he studied the fetching redhead. "How is the investigation going?"

Colbie shifted in her chair, slightly uncomfortable with having to admit the investigation was quickly becoming a bust if something didn't break soon. "It's slower than I like— but, I'm having trouble getting in touch with Gaspar Fischer, and it's imperative I speak with him . . ."

"Gaspar? If you're having trouble getting ahold of him, I suspect he's out of town—or, the country."

"I don't suppose you have a way of getting in touch with him . . ."

"Me? Good heavens, no! Ms. Colleen—if you think Gaspar Fischer had anything to do with Reginald Champagne's death, you're mistaken . . ."

"Why do you say that?"

Bachman smiled, amusement tugging at his lips. "What's his motive? Why would he benefit from Reginald's death?"

Again, Colbie shifted uncomfortably. Those were the questions she couldn't answer and, as far as she could tell, Jan Bachman knew it. "Precisely why I need to speak with Fischer . . . if you can make that happen for me, I'll appreciate it."

Bachman stood, signaling the meeting was over. "Unfortunately, Ms. Colleen, I can't help you. I don't know where he is, or how to get ahold of him . . ."

Colbie took the cue. "Well, if you happen to hear from him . . .

"You'll be the first to know—you have my word."

Colbie took her time heading for the door. She stopped, turning to Bachman, her hand on the door latch. "I suppose you heard about Gregor Hoffer . . ."

Jan Bachman blanched at the mention of Hoffer's name. "Gregor? What about him?"

"Just that he's laid out on a slab at the morgue—the unfortunate recipient of a couple of bullets to the head." Colbie watched him carefully for any signal of guilt or discomfort.

Nothing.

"How do you know?"

Colbie checked her watch. "I'm afraid I'm late for another appointment—again, thank you for your time." With that, she was gone, leaving Jan Bachman mired in tangled thoughts.

****

Brian watched as Colbie pitched her messenger bag on the small, kitchenette table. "No luck, huh?"

"How can you tell?"

"Oh, I don't know—maybe it's the scowl on your face. Or, the damage you inflicted on the table just now . . ."

Colbie grinned. "Funny, Brian . . ."

He clicked off the television, ready to listen. "Seriously—what happened?"

"Not much—although when I mentioned Hoffer's name, Bachman turned a lovely shade of white." She paused as she claimed a spot by Brian on the couch. "Although he says differently, I have no doubt Bachman knows where Fischer is."

Colbie leaned her head back, closing her eyes. Suddenly, the numeral one exploded in her mind's eye, quickly fragmenting and forming again as the church outside of Gruyères.

Instantly, Brian recognized what was happening. "What do you see?"

"The number one—and, the church . . ."

"Another number? What the hell does that mean?"

Colbie opened her eyes, her intuition receding. "It can only mean one thing—the numbers four, seven, and eight were numbers on the list, right? Well, who was number one on that list?"

"Holy shit! Christoph Anderegg! But, I thought he was on our side! When you met with him, did you get any feelings to the contrary?"

Colbie felt a hot flush creep up her neck an face. "No—I didn't have any indication he might be someone other than he seems . . ." Again, she thought of Rifkin sitting across from her at the prison, confidently telling her she was inadequate. Weak. Ineffectual. Not recognizing Anderegg might be more involved than they thought certainly validated his words—at least in her mind.

"Okay—so, now what?"

She thought for a minute, unsure of her answer. "What do you think?"

Brian glanced at her, again recognizing her lack of confidence. "Well—let's look first at who's fate is certain. I think that's Gregor Hoffer since he's indisposed at the morgue."

"True—we're still missing Gaspar Fischer, however. Where the hell is he?"

"I think if Hoffer's whacked, then it's a good possibility Fischer met the same fate . . ."

Colbie sat up straight, her eyes narrowing. "You might be right! It makes sense—no wonder I haven't been able to get ahold of him!"

"You know damned well his employees have instructions to never divulge his whereabouts—chances are good they have no idea, even though he hasn't been around for nearly a month."

"So—no one's found a body. Hoffer was an easy pick, apparently, and whoever decided to do him in really didn't give a rat's ass if he were discovered quickly, or not . . ."

"The definition of arrogance, don't you think?"

Colbie thought about her latest visions. "I saw the number one, and the church. Do you think Fischer could be around the church somewhere?"

Brian's eyes lit up as he considered the question—he was sure he had the answer. "I think he's in that cemetery!"

"You mean whoever got rid of him actually buried him there?"

"That's exactly what I think . . ."

Colbie hesitated. Should she ask?

Brian recognized the look. "I know—you want to go to the church. Now . . ."

"Don't you think it makes sense to scrounge around in the dark? I don't know about you, but I don't feel like getting caught in broad daylight!"

"I don't feel like getting caught, at all . . ."

"Nor do I—so we're better off snooping in the dark . . ."

Within ten minutes, they were out the door, ready to tackle whatever it was they might discover.

For the most part, they drove in silence until they reached Gruyères, both lost in their private thoughts. Brian considered how they were going to get into the church, or comb the cemetery for something illicit. Colbie, however, couldn't think of anything else but her inability to solve the case weeks ago. It used to be she would have a good handle on things within a month or two. But, this case? Well, the truth was if she didn't have Brian with her, she was sure they wouldn't be as far along as they were. He was the one funneling her ideas, and she always followed suit—it was safer that way. Besides, she was learning he was almost always right. When he discovered his intuitive mind was accurate, something changed in her. *Am I jealous*, she wondered as they pulled onto the church's narrow street. It was a question plaguing her for the last weeks and months— ever since his first vision.

Brian eased the car between two vehicles paralleled parked on a side street two blocks over, he and Colbie quietly closing the doors as they got out. Opting for a less obvious route, they skirted the church, finally arriving from the back.

"Okay—now what? Should we see if we can get in?"

Colbie shook her head. "No—I'm thinking you're right about the cemetery. We don't have extra time to waste, so let's get to it . . ."

"Check—what do you have in mind?"

Without answering, Colbie knelt by the grave marker closest to her, placing her palm against the frigid, carved stone. "What does the marker say," she asked Brian as she tried to tune in.

"It's hard to read in the dark—but I think it says, "Marietta Stoler, 1876 - 1910.""

"If she's really buried here, she died young . . ."

"What do you mean, 'if she's really buried here'?"

"I don't feel a thing—no residual life force, and I don't have a sense of anyone's being here . . ."

After a moment, Colbie moved to the adjacent marker, she and Brian going through the same process—she didn't feel anything there, either.

Then, she noticed.

Standing, she glanced at Brian, then pointed. "What do you notice about this grave? What's different?"

It didn't take him long. "Good God—you're right! There isn't snow on this grave, and there is on all the others!"

"Yep—so why is that?"

"Obviously, something—or, somebody—has been here recently . . ."

Colbie nodded. "What else do you notice?"

Brian stared at the grave, then bent down to touch the ragged grass. Then he glanced at the surrounding graves. "This grass is totally different . . ."

"Exactly . . ."

"Fischer?"

"Do you mean Fischer went to the trouble to create a ruse, or is he six feet under?"

"I think he's buried here—that's why you haven't been able to get ahold of him."

Colbie stared at the grave, then at Brian. "If that's the case, we have to bring in the authorities even though it may make our figuring out who killed Reginald Champagne that much more difficult . . ."

"Well, we can't sit on this, that's for sure . . ."

"Why not? All we have is suspicion and, in a cop's eyes, that doesn't amount for much."

"Do you think keeping it from Bollinger is really a good idea?"

Colbie shook her head. "Not really, but you know as well as I do, as soon as we start flapping our jaws, Bollinger will have this place crawling with cops . . ."

"Then, when? We're going to have to bring him in sometime . . ."

"I know—but let's sit on it for a week or so. I have a feeling things are going to bust open if we don't rush it."

Hers was a decision that didn't inspire confidence. Was Colbie making a rash decision? Brian thought it possible— but, he didn't want to diminish her self-respect any further than it was. "Okay—but, only a week or two. I don't think it's wise to stay mum any longer than that . . ."

"Agreed. If we haven't figured out who killed Reginald, we go to Bollinger . . ." For a second, she wondered if she were making the right decision.

But, she knew it was the right thing to do.

****

"What did she say?"

"Nothing really—only questions about Gaspar Fischer, and do I know where he is . . ."

Christoph Anderegg stared at Jan Bachman, unsure if he answered the investigator's questions well enough to derail her. "Well? What did you tell her?"

"The usual—I said I didn't know, but if she couldn't find him, he is most likely out of town, or the country."

"Was that lame answer enough to shut her up?"

"Until she was leaving . . ." Bachman nervously fidgeted in his chair.

"What does that mean?

"She asked if I knew of Hoffer's demise—said he was slapped on a gurney in the morgue."

Anderegg's face exploded, anger flushing every feature. "She knows!"

Bachman shook his head. "How could she know? Up until this moment, she hasn't been all that bright—clues have been right in front of her, and she hasn't really figured anything out. She so much as told me the case is dead unless she can find Fischer . . ."

Anderegg fell silent, thinking of each way things could go wrong. If discovered, it would be the end of his personal empire, and that was something he just couldn't allow. "Get Harold over here—if he gives you any trouble, take care of him . . ."

Bachman nodded, understanding perfectly. "When do you want to see him?"

Christoph leveled a disbelieving look at his only true minion. "Yesterday . . ."

****

Turns out Harold Remington wasn't that easy to find. When he should be in his office, Bachman kept getting the run around by Remington's secretary. He had to admit, she was good—she left him no room to be nosy. Not only that, if he had to report to Anderegg within the next twenty-four hours and he couldn't locate Remington—well, it was a thought he didn't relish.

There were a couple of Remington haunts he knew about, one being Tropical Islands not too far from home. He was there only once, a guest of Fischer and Remington—and, with any luck, he still had the number of the hotel where they stayed in his contacts list. *It's worth a try*, he thought, as he scrolled through a length list. Finally, pay dirt. *Aha! I thought so!* He dialed, waiting for anyone to answer—even a non-human.

He was in luck. "Tropical Islands Hotel," a pleasant voice answered.

"Harold Remington, please . . ."

"One moment . . ."

Bachman couldn't believe it! If Remington actually answered, he knew he would meet his boss's orders. If not? It would be on to Plan B—a trip to Tropical Islands.

Remington's voice interrupted his thoughts. "Remington."

"Harold—Jan Bachman. Anderegg wants to see you immediately . . ." Bachman could hear Remington sigh.

"About what?"

"I don't think that's for me to say—all I know is he gave me orders to have you in his office no later than tomorrow."

By then, Remington's temper took root. "I don't answer to him! Who the hell does that S.O.B. think he is?"

Bachman smiled, glad Remington couldn't see him.

"He's your boss, Harold—and, you know it. I hate to think of the ramifications if you choose to ignore his orders . . ."

Silence.

Moments passed as Remington tried to figure a way out, but it wasn't to be. "Tell him I'll be there at three o'clock—it's the best I can do."

Bachman smirked, thinking about how quickly Remington acquiesced. "I think you're doing the right thing, Harold—he'll see you tomorrow at three."

Both men clicked off at the same time, each consumed by differing thoughts. Bachman wasn't sure what Anderegg had in mind, but he knew it wasn't going to be pleasant for Remington. When Christoph Anderegg was involved, things had a way of turning when least expected.

For a brief moment, he felt sorry for the arrogant bank exec.

But, only a brief moment.

CHAPTER TWENTY-FOUR

C hristoph Anderegg was seldom accepted into societal norms—and, he refused to apologize for it. Ever since he could remember, he stepped outside the fringes, even in primary school. Kids laughed at him for reasons he couldn't understand and, as he progressed through the education system, things didn't get much better. He did, however, find a group of friends with whom he could be himself, but those allegiances were fleeting, and he decided to bounce from grade to grade, steeled and friendless.

It wasn't until he attended university he decided to reinvent himself.

During those years, relationships were non-existent. Not that he didn't try—the young women his age, however, exhibited little to no interest and, again, he found himself going it alone. But, that was okay—the plans he made for his future didn't include a wife and a couple of kids. No—he was much more interested in making it to the top. Being rich. Being powerful. The problem was his personality didn't fit in with the big guns of business, especially banking. But when Harold Remington was hired at Reginald Champagne's bank, Anderegg recognized the sweet sound of change.

From the beginning, Anderegg observed, Remington proved himself to be a self-absorbed, loud-mouthed lout, taking advantage of women as well as any situation in which he could make money. Rumor had it he had a wife back in the States, but Anderegg couldn't speak to its veracity. All he knew was the young man traveled from the States to Zurich, and only one time could Anderegg recall the woman on Remington's arm being his wife. Other times? Well—you can imagine. High-priced and elegant, they adorned him like a fine piece of expensive jewelry, and Harold Remington loved every second of it.

It really was no surprise his marriage didn't last.

Fortunately, a failing marriage didn't make any difference to Anderegg—Harold Remington wasn't a part of his plan, so what did it matter? But, as odd as Remington was to the likes of the Swiss banking magnate, he made the perfect partner. Shrewd. Spoiled. Servile. Just what Christoph needed for his fledgling, underground enterprise—and, before he knew it, Harold Remington was a part of his operation. With the understanding, of course, Anderegg was completely in charge. He didn't need someone snapping orders at him—he needed someone who would acquiesce.

A fact apparently lost on Mr. Remington.

Christoph Anderegg's first underground deal occurred purely by happenstance—a 'right place at the right time' kind of thing. A friend of a friend introduced him to a long-time—legit—arms dealer years ago and, ever since, his bank account thanked him for doing business. Then, things became not so legit—a different kind of team was born. Throughout the years Christoph and Harold learned the soft approach was seldom best, and something more intimidating was in order—which was just fine with them. So, one thing led to another and, within the decade, Anderegg assembled a small, elite group who would carry out his orders with minimal supervision. Gaspar Fisher, Jan Bachman, and Gregor Hoffer would answer to Harold Remington, and Remington would answer directly to Anderegg—another fact lost on Mr. Remington.

How he despised pecking orders . . .

****

The only table left was in the back, not too far from the kitchen's swinging doors. It wasn't perfect, but it would have to do—as hungry as they were, Colbie and Brian didn't care where they ate.

"I can't remember being this hungry in a long time," Colbie confessed as she slid into the slippery booth.

"Same here—I think I'll have the same thing I had last week . . ."

"Fondue? How about if we split it, and then order

something else? I want to get as much Swiss food in me as I can before we leave!" Colbie chuckled, noticing Brian was fiddling with his belt buckle.

"I only have one more hole left—I'll have to buy a bigger belt!"

"That's okay—I'll still love you!"

Brian sipped his wine, silent for several moments. "Speaking of leaving—do you have any idea of when that's going to be?"

Colbie shook her head. "Nothing definite, but I have a feeling we're going to bust things open soon . . ."

"Really? I'm surprised you think we're that close—after Hoffer's murder, I'm not sure what direction we're going."

Colbie looked at him, knowing he was being more truthful than she. As much as she wanted to be at the point where the case would almost solve itself, it simply wasn't so—and, Brian knew it. "Sometimes, neither do I . . ." She paused, taking a sip of her cocktail. "Brian?"

It was a tone he hadn't heard for a long time. "What?"

"There's something we need to discuss . . ."

"Which is?"

Again, Colbie paused, sucking in a deep breath before launching into something she knew Brian wouldn't want to hear. "Remember when we were getting ready to leave for Switzerland?"

Brian nodded.

"And, do you remember when I got home that one night, I didn't feel well? I know you were worried about me . . ."

Brian recalled the evening all too well. "I remember—and, you're right. I was worried about you . . ." He watched as she looked down at the table as though she were completely embarrassed. Reaching across the table, he took her hand. "What is it you want to tell me?"

Colbie swallowed hard. "Well—that was the day I went to see Rifkin in prison . . ."

He tried to squelch a rising anger. "What? Why?"

"Because I thought if I visited him, I might . . ." Her voice caught as she recalled the conversation.

"You might what?"

"Feel as if I'm worth something—he always admired my abilities, and I needed closure. He was someone I looked up to . . ."

Brian sat quietly, trying to digest what he was hearing. "Call me thick, but I don't think I understand—did you get what you wanted?"

Now it was Colbie's turn to be quiet until she ramped up a little more courage. "No—all he did was verify why I visited him in the first place. He called me weak. He said I was wrestling with the fact I didn't know who he really was—and is. It was like a slap in the face, but I knew he was right. Somehow, some way, I need to forgive myself for not seeing the truth about him." She hesitated. "How could I have been so wrong?"

Tears welled, and Brian gave her hand a squeeze. "Hey—it's Rifkin. Obviously, he's one of the best cons to grace the planet. I'm sure you aren't the only one he's screwed over . . ."

"That may be, but he screwed me—and, I can't seem to get over it!"

Brian said nothing. He knew she was about to erupt and, when she did, he wasn't quite sure what he should do.

"Haven't you noticed?" Colbie's voice pitched higher. "Haven't you noticed I can't even trust my visions now? Who knows if what I'm seeing is the truth?"

The first tear.

"Well, if I'm going to be honest—as we promised each other we always will be—I did notice a change in your behavior. But, I didn't know it was because of Rifkin . . ."

"Neither did I, until I saw him that day. He corroborated how I was feeling . . . it was like he looked inside my soul, delighting in telling me everything that's wrong with me!" She dabbed at her eyes with the corner of her napkin.

Brian leaned back in his chair, hating the sorrow etched on her face. "I have an idea—how about if we ask the waitress to box up our food, and we'll eat in our room? What do you think?"

All Colbie could do was nod.

****

Harold Remington arrived precisely at three o'clock. "I told Bachman I'd be here," he advised Anderegg, "and I'm a man of my word . . ."

"I appreciate that, Harold—both of us are busy, and it's always best we make good use of our time . . ." Anderegg gestured toward the small bar in his office. "Drink?" He noticed Harold was still standing. "Please—have a seat."

"Thank you—no." He paused as he chose a designer chair close to the window. "I have a meeting soon, so perhaps we should discuss why you summoned me."

"Summoned you? That has an ominous tone, don't you think?"

"Indeed, I do . . . so, why did you summon me?"

Anderegg made the most of a pregnant pause. "As you know, Harold, we've made quite a success of our little business—and, I appreciate your efforts."

"Does this mean I'm getting a raise?"

Christoph shot him a look. "No reason to be flip, Harold—no, you're not getting a raise. Unfortunately, it's just the opposite. I feel, at this time in my life, it's prudent for me to downsize . . ."

"Downsize? What the hell does that mean?"

"I decided to end our operation—you know, before things get sticky."

Harold sat, staring at him in disbelief. Did Christoph Anderegg really think he could simply dismiss him without repercussions? Clearly, he hadn't given the consequences much thought. "I'm afraid it's not that easy," he commented, careful not to break eye contact.

"Ah—I thought that might be your take. But, it really is that easy—I already notified our contacts our pending deal will be our last and, if nothing else, I let them know you'll no longer be representing our organization. I let them know you're dismissed . . ."

That did it. Harold erupted, anger consuming him. "Dismissed?"

"Well, yes—I think that describes your position as of now quite well, don't you think?"

Harold made an effort to calm himself. "This seems rather sudden—it's strange you're making this decision as a private investigator is nosing around. What does she have to do with it?"

"You must mean Colbie Colleen—the truth is I haven't given her much thought. Although, I heard she's sniffing around your neck of the woods—your ex-wife's hiring her probably has something to do with it. You must admit, it was incredibly stupid . . ."

Remington didn't say anything—Anderegg was right. Colbie Colleen's investigation didn't sit well with him, and he could well imagine it didn't sit well with Christoph. *Is that what this is about? An investigator who hasn't been able to solve who killed Reginald Champagne?* He could understand why Anderegg was upset, but was that any reason to shut everything down? "If it's Colbie Colleen you're worried about," he offered, "I can take care of that piece of business before you can spit . . ."

A smile. "I'm afraid it's not quite that easy . . ."

Right then, Remington became fully aware his association with Christoph Anderegg was over—at least as far as Anderegg was concerned.

For Remington, it wasn't quite that cut and dried.

****

"I can't give you anything concrete—it's a feeling."

From what Lieutenant Bollinger knew of Colbie, she didn't strike him as one to give him a line of B.S. "So," he began as he leaned back in his chair, "you're telling me you think the cemetery at the stone church outside of Gruyères has something to do with your case, and mine. That being, of course, who murdered Reginald Champagne. What I don't get is why you think they're connected . . ."

"Because from the beginning of our time in Zurich, the church has been at the forefront of our investigation. Think about it—the pastor's mysterious suicide? Nicole Remington's murder? Our seeing Gaspar Fischer watching a grave being filled in?"

Bollinger hadn't heard about that. "Okay—let's assume the cemetery holds clues. What do you want me to do?"

Colbie glanced at the door to make certain it was closed. "I want you to dig up one of the graves . . ."

Bollinger suppressed his desire to send her on her way— he didn't have time for a costly exhumation. "I'm afraid that's impossible . . ."

"Why? I'll bet you can get the paperwork submitted by tomorrow . . ."

The police Lieutenant scooted his chair forward. She was right—all he had to do was get it going. As he considered her suggestion, he also considered the possibility of Colbie's giving up on the idea—it wasn't good. "Alright—we'll try to get an exhumation. But, that's an old cemetery—getting permission can take a long time."

Colbie grinned. "Maybe, but I don't think it will—I also have the feeling things are going to move quickly . . ."

"I hope so, Ms. Colleen—I hope so."

CHAPTER TWENTY-FIVE

—————❖—————

Jan Bachman sank into his favorite chair, drink in hand, thinking about the events of the week. Anderegg's firing Harold Remington? That was rich! And, Hoffer? Well, his demise was the icing on the cake—Hoffer had been getting on his nerves and, as far as Bachman could tell, his not being around didn't complicate things. In fact, everything was progressing smoothly. He was comforted by the fact the operation was trimmed to only two people—Anderegg, and him. Yes, Remington was still going to be a pain in the ass, but, what bothered him was the ease with which his former boss was canned—it wasn't a far stretch to think the same thing might happen to him.

Or, worse.

It was the 'or, worse' part that laid the foundation for

Plan B. He knew damned well Remington wasn't going to take his dismissal without a fight, and he also knew from all of his years answering to Harold, a simmering rage would eventually erupt—of that, he was certain. *So, he thought, why not get Remington out of the picture? Why wait for him to strike with revenge?*

As the sun dipped behind the financial district's highrise buildings—and, a few cocktails later—his thoughts turned to Nicole. She was, in his mind, the epitome of a woman—strong. Confident. Classy. He wouldn't have minded a more permanent relationship, but she made it clear she was only interested in what he could do for her in the money department.

Turned out, he could do plenty.

Over the years her nest egg grew, Bachman entrenching himself in all facets of her life. There wasn't a thing he didn't know about her, and he regarded her part in the kidnapping situation and subsequent incarceration as things to be admired. When it came to money, they were a perfect match.

Five minutes later, he drained his glass in darkness.

It's such a shame I had to kill her . . .

****

"Bollinger just called—they received permission for the exhumation. That's if there's a body buried there, at all . . ."

"When?" Brian set his laptop on the coffee table, knowing they were going to be out the door.

"Now—he asked us to meet him at the cemetery." Colbie pulled on her Wellies, then grabbed her coat. "C'mon—I don't want to miss a thing!"

Brian called down to the valet, and ten minutes later they were one their way to the city's perimeter—within two hours, they parked in front of the vintage church. "There's Bollinger," Colbie commented as they approached the cemetery. "A couple of officers are already digging . . ."

"Weird—you think he would have brought in a backhoe, or something . . ."

"I thought the same thing—his way is a little less obvious, though. The last thing he needs is a bunch of people gawking . . ."

Bollinger motioned for them to join him. "We just got started . . ." He glanced at Colbie. "I hope you're right . . ."

Colbie touched the gravestone, waiting for her intuitive senses to kick in. Within seconds, visions filled her mind. "Oh, I'm right—I don't have any doubt about that!"

The officers didn't have to dig too far—a few feet down, feet appeared, clad in expensive shoes and socks. A few minutes later, a body lay exposed in front of them.

"That's what I thought," Colbie commented as the officers revealed a face. "That's Gaspar Fischer . . ."

****

By dusk, the cemetery was labeled a crime scene, cordoned off with police tape while Lieutenant Bollinger argued with someone on the other end of his cell. "I know it's a strange request, but I need clearance as of yesterday!"He clicked off, muttering about the ineptitude of the small town's administrative force.

He turned to Colbie. "Tell me what you know about Fischer . . ."

"I don't know much, really—other than he was Harold Remington's right-hand man. But, I always had the feeling he was responsible for Reginald's death—or, at least, he had something to do with it."

"Do you think he pulled the trigger?"

Colbie shook her head. "No—especially now because he's stretched out in front of us. If he were responsible for Reginald's, Nicole's, or Hoffer's murders, he wouldn't be here, don't you think?"

Brian glanced at Colbie, then Bollinger. "You do realize there are only two people on our list who are still alive—Bachman and Anderegg. The way I see it, it's a pretty good bet that Christoph Anderegg is the guy dishing out orders."

"Well, not the entire list—only numbers four, seven, and eight. And, don't forget Harold Remington—he's still in the mix . . ."

"True—but, I'm thinking Anderegg is our 'top of the pyramid' guy. He has the prestige and power to run an illegal weapons operation—and, I'll bet Fischer, Bachman, and

Hoffer worked for him outside of their professional confines."

"What about Reginald," Colbie asked. "Do you think Anderegg is responsible for his murder?"

Brian hesitated. If he were wrong . . . "Yes—I do. I think Reginald was involved with his underground operation, and called him on it—he didn't like the way things were going."

"That's something that probably wouldn't sit well with Anderegg," Colbie commented.

"That's what I think—I also think Jan Bachman is his trigger man. He's the only one who's remained under our radar until recently . . ."

"But, why would Anderegg want those guys dead? He stands to make more money if they're alive . . ."

"Because," Bollinger answered, "he wants everything for himself." He eyed Colbie. "Trust me—if what you and Brian think is true, Jan Bachman should be watching his back . . ."

As Colbie listened to Brian's thoughts about the Reginald Champagne investigation, she realized his ideas were far ahead of hers, and he seemed to have a much better handle on how the pieces fit. "But, what about Nicole? I think she was involved only because of the money—who killed her?"

Again, Brian took the lead. "Bachman—I think he's really an Anderegg sycophant, and he'll do whatever Anderegg tells him."

By the time they wrapped up for the evening, Colbie stood on the fringe of her shadow world. The thought of her inability to run her investigation successfully thrashed in her mind and, if she were honest with herself, Brian was the one laying bare how several murders pieced together. *That's my job,* she scolded herself as she stepped into her comfort zone.

But, that still leaves Harold Remington . . .

****

He swished his cocktail, forcing ice cubes stuck together to clink on the sides of the glass. *Perhaps I made a mistake,* Harold thought as he considered his position. *But, they pissed me off, and I couldn't let such disrespect go unnoticed. It wouldn't be right . . .* His biggest regret, however, was letting Gaspar Fischer go. Even though Fischer's dramatic flair rankled his last nerve every time they were together, he was good at what he did. Bachman and Hoffer? He could have cared less about them . . .

For Harold, the question became what was he going to do about Anderegg—and, Bachman. Throughout the years, he never considered being pushed aside, and he sure as hell didn't believe Anderegg was going to shut down the operation—doing so would go against everything Harold knew about the Swiss banker. As far back as he could recall, Anderegg proved himself to be interested in one thing— money. A motivator Harold knew well. Anderegg would do anything to get it, and those impeding his progress toward a goal of being filthy rich would land them somewhere they didn't want to be. Knowing that, Harold deemed Anderegg's walking away from a lucrative underground operation didn't jive with what Anderegg told him.

Then there was Jan Bachman. His size a deterrent to

most, Harold knew he was really a snowflake. Given the right set of circumstances, Bachman would throw anyone under the bus, and he'd sing his heart out given a chance. But, was he really a threat to Harold?

You bet he was.

Anderegg and Bachman together? To Harold, Bachman was worrisome—it appeared he was taking his place. But, what could he do? Due to his unfortunate dismissal, getting his foot in the door with either man could be tricky. Perhaps a better plan would be to work Anderegg first—he might be willing to schedule an early dinner with him to discuss the dissolution of their operation. *It's worth a try, anyway,* he thought as he took one last sip.

It's always worth a try . . .

****

Colbie took off her glasses, her eyes focusing on something Brian couldn't see. "Anderegg," she muttered. "Something's changed . . ."

"What's changed?" Brian didn't take his eyes from the computer screen.

"Relationships . . ."

He glanced up, the look on her face telling him he should pay attention. "What kind of relationships—personal? Business?"

Colbie tried to hone in on exactly what she was seeing. "Business. I also see the front doors of what looks like a restaurant . . ."

"Can you see the name on it?"

"No, but it looks familiar."

Brian paused a moment, then gently prodded her for more information. The fact was he was growing weary of Switzerland, the case, and he was ready to head back to the States. "Have you been there?" Again, he paused. "Have we been there?"

Colbie sat up straight, her eyes lighting up. "That's it! Yes—I met Gaspar Fischer there!"

"Excellent! What do you think it means?"

Colbie sat back against the couch cushions as her visions faded. "We're supposed to go there for some reason . . ."

"When?"

"Now . . ."

Brian bounced up and grabbed her hand. "Then let's go! I'm starving!"

****

The restaurant looked as tired in the evening as it had during the day. Dim lights meant to invite patrons did more to scare them away—except for the locals. They knew it had the best food in Zurich.

"This reminds me of the steakhouse back home," Colbie mentioned as they got settled. "Remember? They had the best prime rib ever!"

Brian chuckled at the memory. "I do remember—we had to go once a month so you could get your fix . . ."

After a quick glance at the menu, both decided on the daily special, then sat back to watch the comings and goings. Colbie had her back to the front door—they figured Brian would be less noticed and recognizable. "I was tuning in on the way here," she mentioned as the server brought their drinks.

"Anything worthwhile?"

Colbie shook her head. "Not really . . ."

Just as she took a sip of her cocktail, she glanced at Brian, his eyebrows arched with disbelief. "What? What's going on?" She tried to keep her composure, even though she wanted to turn around.

"You're never gonna believe who just walked through the door . . ."

"Don't keep me in suspense! Who!"

"Christoph Anderegg . . ."

"Holy shit! You're kidding!"

Brian shook his head. "Thank God you have your back to the front door . . ."

Colbie tried to look as inconspicuous as possible. "I hope they don't seat him near us," she whispered as Brian watched the hostess show him to his table.

"He's at a table close to the front . . ."

"Does he have a good view of us?"

"No—he'd have to turn his head to see our table."

Both were silent before Colbie suggested a plan. "He doesn't know what you look like, and you're in a good position to monitor his movements. Telling me what's happening will look like we're engaged in conversation . . ."

Brian agreed. "He took a table for four—obviously, he's meeting someone . . ."

"He doesn't strike me as the type of guy who likes to be kept waiting, so whoever he's meeting will probably show up soon."

Colbie was right. A few minutes later, Brian glanced at the front entrance. "It's Remington—it's freakin' Harold Remington!"

Brian continued to watch as the hostess led Remington to Anderegg's table. No handshakes. No smiles. Harold removed his coat, placing it carefully on the chair to his left as Anderegg seemed to be interested in the menu. They spoke little until the server took their order, then headed for the kitchen. "Here's my question—I know they're colleagues, but, from the look of it, this doesn't look like a friendly meeting."

From his vantage point, Brian thought he noticed a florid flush creeping up Anderegg's neck. "He looks pissed!"

"Who?"

"Anderegg! And, Harold kind of looks like a whipped puppy . . ."

Colbie thought for a moment. "That tells me Anderegg holds a position of authority over Harold . . ."

Brian nodded. "I told you I think he's the top guy on the pyramid . . ."

The 'I told you so' stung a little, but he was right—he figured it out long before she did. "You're right, of course . . ."

He instantly regretted the gentle dig. "Don't be too hard on yourself—we're a team, and it really doesn't make any difference who thought what first."

Colbie nodded. "You're right, again—besides, this is no time for me to feel sorry for myself!"

The server delivered their entrées, then made a beeline for the hostess stand. By the time she returned to their table, only a few remnants of steak remained. "You must have been hungry," she exclaimed. "What would you like for dessert?"

Brian and Colbie laughed, and shook their heads. "None for us! We're stuffed!"

Moments later they had their check, Brian taking his time to pay. Anderegg and Remington looked as if they were embroiled in a fiery conversation, and the investigators didn't want to miss a thing.

Suddenly, Remington grabbed his coat and stood, shooting a serious look at his colleague before he turned to leave. Brian noticed Anderegg's left hand gripping the side of his chair as Remington headed toward the front entrance. "I think Anderegg is trying not to lose it—he's really pissed! So is Remington . . ."

Shortly after Harold left, Anderegg tossed cash on the table before striding toward the entrance. Brian watched, until both men were clearly out of sight. "Okay—they're gone . . ."

Colbie turned toward the front. "What table?"

"That one . . ." Brian pointed.

"Okay—I'm going to visit the ladies' room . . ." Brian stood as she got up, watching her closely as she approached Anderegg's table. It was the perfect ruse to get a good look at anything either man might have left behind.

A few minutes later, she returned, again glancing at the table as she passed. Nothing of their meeting was left, the table wiped and set with napkins and silverware for the next patrons.

"Anything?"

"Nope—nothing."

Brian handed Colbie her coat. "Let's get out of here—based on what we just witnessed, I think we need to regroup and focus our attention on Anderegg and Remington. I have a feeling things are coming to a head . . ."

Colbie nodded. "I know they are . . ."

CHAPTER TWENTY-SIX

———————❖———————

Mistakes made by Christoph Anderegg were unusual—he seldom made them, and he refused to tolerate those who did, especially his own colleagues. So, when he learned authorities busted members of a top gang in Zurich, he was sweating a little more than usual. He knew Remington conducted business with such unsavory types—keeping their identities to himself—and, he also knew if Harold's contacts were swept up in the bust, trouble brewed.

Remington's allegiances were sketchy, at best.

It was Bachman who dropped the bombshell—he had his ear to the pavement twenty-four hours a day. There was little he didn't know and, after learning of the gang bust, he didn't waste any time hot-footing it to his boss. Of course, he had to ferret out names included in the bust which took a little time, but within a few hours he was confident he could go to Anderegg with pertinent information before it hit the wires.

"Are you sure," Anderegg asked. "You may have made a mistake . . ." But, in his gut, he knew that wouldn't be the case—Bachman was too anal to come to him with volatile information.

"No mistake—shall I tell Remington?"

Anderegg paced for a few minutes before answering. "No—let's wait to see what Remington does. If he knows of the apprehension, he'll come unglued—that's when he'll make a fatal mistake. We can take care of things then . . ."

Bachman stared at his boss. "Are you sure? He's damned pissed about your taking him off the payroll—who knows what he'll say or do!"

"True—but it's a risk we'll have to take . . ."

"What about the investigators? They'll hear of this, that's for sure . . ."

Bachman's question was a sore spot with Anderegg—over the last few days, concern about Colbie Colleen and her partner mounted. When Anderegg first met her, she was nothing more than an annoyance. Now? He wasn't so sure—a needling feeling told him she was making more progress on Reginald's murder than she let on. *If,* he thought, *she has doubts about me, there's no telling what she'll do.*

He was right.

****

As soon as Bollinger told Colbie and Brian about the bust—particularly its leader, Gian Caflisch—they were on the lieutenant's doorstep within the hour. He invited them to view the interview, grabbing two extra chairs as they prepared to settle in front of the closed circuit monitor ten minutes before Caflisch was escorted into the room on the other side of the glass. Colbie watched as the new inmate took a chair directly across from Lieutenant Bollinger. *He's tough*, she thought as he sat down.

It took awhile, but Caflisch eventually spilled—although not about everything—and, by the time they called it a day late that evening, Colbie had a good handle on who killed Reginald Champagne. She wasn't one hundred percent certain, but when she and Brian briefly discussed the possibility of who pulled the trigger, her certainty increased.

"Meet me in my office," Bollinger requested as he exited the interview room. "I'll be there shortly . . ." Several minutes later, he sat at his desk, flipping through his notes."So—I have my own ideas. What do you think?" He glanced at Colbie and Brian.

Colbie took the lead. "Well, he mentioned only two names, and nothing about Anderegg. As we suspected, Bachman and Remington were joined at the hip . . ."

"I think Remington doesn't—or, didn't—have a clue Bachman is really working for Anderegg," Brian offered, "and everything Bachman did or said really came from Christoph. They played Remington like a fiddle . . ."

"Until, of course, Anderegg cut ties with Remington . . ."

"True—but, there's one other person we haven't taken into consideration. Who killed Gregor Hoffer?"

Colbie tapped her pencil on the side of her chair, thinking about the elite group of banking execs who chose greed over respect. "I think Harold put a hit on Hoffer . . ."

"The guy Bollinger just arrested?" Brian glanced at the lieutenant who was taking notes on a yellow legal pad.

"At first, yes—but, I have a feeling that job was handed to someone else."

"If that's the case," Bollinger suggested, "he'll probably start singing as soon as we pick him up—any thoughts on who that is?"

"No—it's just a feeling . . ."

Bollinger smiled slightly. "Well, from what I can tell, your feelings have been pretty accurate."

Colbie appreciated the lieutenant's comment—it helped assuage her self-doubt. "Thanks—but we still have some work to do. What do you think about setting up Anderegg? I can schedule another meeting with him to see if I can get additional information about Reginald . . ."

Brian glanced at Bollinger. "I don't know about that—we know Anderegg can't be trusted. Besides, who's to say he'll see you?"

Colbie recalled her two brief meetings with him early in their investigation, both yielding little information—but, what she couldn't figure out was why Anderegg whispered the clue about numbers four, seven, and eight. When she voiced her question to Bollinger and Brian, the answer was obvious. "Because," Bollinger suggested, "he wanted to steer the investigation away from him. He clearly has no problem ratting anyone out in order to save his own skin . . ."

As soon as the words left Bollinger's mouth, Colbie silently chastised herself for not seeing what was right in front of her. "You're right, but I think he'll be curious—I'm pretty sure he's going to try to figure out how much we know. It's his nature to always be on top—he didn't get where he is by being stupid."

"Agreed." Again, Bollinger flipped through his notes. "Go ahead, then—try to set an appointment with him. I'll make sure we have your back . . ."

Colbie and Brian walked down the steps shortly after ten, each thinking about the danger involved by Colbie's putting herself in front of Anderegg for a third time.

Things could get dicey.

****

Turns out Harold did know about the bust, and he was none to happy about it. He still had a fraction of faith, however—gang members weren't known for spilling their guts, and being labeled a snitch would surely be the end of things. Still, he harbored a modicum of doubt—no matter what he thought, he could be wrong. More concerning was the possibility Caflisch fingered him for the hit list—if that happened, it signaled the end of life as Harold knew it.

The problem was he no longer had anyone left in what was quickly becoming a puny arms operation. It was, indeed, a mistake to fire Fischer, Hoffer, and Bachman—now, he was in the whole mess up to his eyeballs with no one to follow his commands—it left him little in the way of personal protection.

Anderegg doesn't know how lucky he is, Remington thought as he contemplated his next move. Anderegg was next on the list, but, with Caflisch in detention, he'd have to come up with a different plan—which, of course, would include a tad of blackmail because Harold knew who was responsible for Reginald's murder. The truth was he knew all along. *Is Anderegg off police radar? Maybe. Chances are good after months of stagnation, they have no idea who killed Reginald Champagne . . .*

The bigger question was did Anderegg know Remington had anything to hold over his head? Possibly, but doubtful. Anderegg was arrogant enough to think he got away with it—after all, the cops only showed up on his doorstep once, never to be seen again.

Harold chuckled, thinking he was in a position of power to take what he wanted. What he craved. What he needed.

Oh, the thoughts of fools . . .

****

"Mr. Anderegg will be with you momentarily . . ."

"Thank you . . ." Colbie took a seat just close enough to the reception desk so she could hear at least one side of a conversation should anyone call, but the switchboard was silent. *Oh, well,* she thought. *It was worth a try . . .*

She didn't have to wait long—five minutes later she sat in front of Christoph Anderegg, eager to begin her interview. "Who would have thought I'd need to see you again," she laughed as she placed a legal pad and pen on her lap. Yes, it was an intimidating move, but she laughed that off, too. "As I get older, I find I can't remember anything unless I write it down—I hope you don't mind!"

"Of course not—I know the feeling." Anderegg paused. "I confess I'm puzzled why you need to see me—I don't know any more than I did when you interviewed me the second time . . ."

Colbie nodded. "I figured that—what I really want to do is throw a few ideas at you to see what you think."

"I'm flattered . . ."

"Let's start with Gaspar Fischer, Gregor Hoffer, and Jan Bachman—numbers four, seven, and eight on the list I showed you during our first meeting. I'm sure you remember telling me to keep my eyes open when it came to them . . ."

"I remember, indeed. A shame Fischer and Hoffer met an—untimely—end."

Colbie eyed him carefully. "Do you know who murdered either of them?"

"No, although I have my suspicions . . ." Anderegg met her gaze without blinking.

"Who would that be?"

"I don't think it's prudent for me to say . . . I may be incorrect."

Colbie scribbled notes for a few seconds. "Ever heard of someone named Gian Caflisch?"

"Caflisch? No . . . the name doesn't sound familiar."

"Then you don't know about the gang bust by authorities a few days ago?"

Anderegg shifted slightly in his chair. "I do know about it—but, what does that have to do with me?"

"Nothing, really—but, from what I understand, he dropped a few names during his interview . . ."

He tried to look interested instead of alarmed. "I assume you know those names?"

"Oh, yes—unfortunately, I'm not at liberty to share them with you."

Anderegg focused his stare on Colbie. "I understand— but, if you can't share those names with me, I'm still not certain why you're here . . ."

Bomb number one. "Reginald Champagne, Mr. Anderegg. Reginald Champagne. I need you to be truthful about what you know . . ."

"And, what makes you think I haven't been truthful?"

Colbie laughed aloud. "Oh, please—you know damned well you threw me a bone, and I chomped on it. What you don't realize is you were on my radar from the beginning." A slight exaggeration, but Anderegg didn't need to know that.

Her admission was exactly what Anderegg didn't want to hear—he suspected as much. "Smugness doesn't become you, Ms. Colleen. Of course I knew I was within your sites, but I have nothing to fear. All I know is what I told you—which was I believed Reginald had enemies on the inside and outside of banking . . ."

Gloves off. "Are you one of those inside enemies?"

Anderegg's knuckles whitened as he gripped the side of his chair. "Why would I have anything to do with Reginald's murder? What could I possibly have to gain?"

Colbie smiled. "Only total control of an underground arms operation . . ."

"Underground arms? Surely, you must be joking!"

"Unfortunately, I'm not—and, I know Harold Remington was in on it. Fischer, Hoffer, and Bachman, too . . ."

That's when everything unraveled.

****

It was time.

Harold decided if he didn't move first, he'd be the one regretting it. Christoph Anderegg wouldn't waste a moment if he felt his business—his life—were on a tightrope. Then he certainly wouldn't hesitate to take care of business to get things back on track. Knowing Anderegg like he did, Remington figured a last conversation was in order, not that it would do any good. Once Anderegg made a decision, that was it—sweet talking him to get back on the payroll wasn't going to work. No—it was time for something more . . .

Drastic.

After checking his weapon one last time, Harold Remington headed for the building in which he'd spent half of his life. He knew every inch of it, so getting to Anderegg surreptitiously would be simple—the crapshoot was his secretary. She had a buzzer under her desk to alert her boss if something were concerning or awry, and she'd use it given half a chance. So, with that in mind, at precisely eleven o'clock, he strode into Christoph Anderegg's outer office with an engaging, ear-to-ear grin.

"Good morning, Mr. Remington!" Then, a sudden look of concern. "I don't have you down for an appointment today—did I miss something?"

"Good morning, Tina! Good heavens, no! I just need to see Christoph for a moment, and I'll be out of your hair."

"He has someone with him at the moment . . ."

Remington shot her his best smile. "I'll be two seconds, I promise!" Without waiting for permission, he winked at Tina, then opened Christoph Anderegg's office door. The first thing he saw?

Colbie Colleen.

Colbie turned as the door opened, stunned at her luck—it couldn't have been any better. "Mr. Remington! How nice to see you! We were just about to discuss matters in which you may be interested—please, come in!"

Well, there were two things Anderegg didn't like—first, it was his office, and how dare she take control? Second, Remington was the last person he wanted to see.

Harold couldn't hide the shocked look on his face. Colbie Colleen? *What the hell is she doing here,* he wondered as he struggled for something to say. After a few silent seconds, he found his voice. "Ms. Colleen—I didn't expect to see you." He glanced at Anderegg. "So sorry, Christoph—I didn't mean to interrupt . . ."

"Oh, you didn't interrupt! Please, have a seat—I think you'll find this interesting . . ." Colbie gestured to the chair next to her.

Harold noticed Anderegg's hand reaching under his desk. *Just in case,* he thought as he took a chair next to Colbie. "Okay, Ms. Colleen—what's so important? I can't imagine you and Christoph were talking about anything to do with me . . ."

Colbie's voice turned cold. "Ah, but we were. It very much has to do with you . . ." She paused, assessing the two men's discomfort. "I suppose," she continued, "you didn't think I would figure it out—who murdered Reginald Champagne, I mean. And, for a while, you were right . . ." Colbie focused on Anderegg. "Especially when you attempted to throw me off track by giving up your most trusted confidants."

"Giving up?" Harold shot a steely stare at Anderegg. "What does she mean by that?"

Anderegg didn't flinch. "Only that . . ."

"Only that," Colbie interrupted, "he threw Fischer, Hoffer, and Bachman under the bus by putting me on their tails. Yours, too, by proxy . . ."

Anderegg didn't move.

"Mine?" Harold's voice was tinged with a slight squeal. "I didn't do anything! Besides, if I had, you would have heard it from Nicole—she didn't waste any time bad mouthing me every time she got the chance."

Colbie managed a wry smile. "That's true—I learned of your contentious relationship early in my investigation. That's why it wasn't a stretch for me to figure out you decided to get rid of Nicole at the hands of Jan Bachman."

Remington squirmed in his seat. "Why would I do that?"

"Oh, it's really pretty simple—Nicole threatened your underground arms operation. She wanted her fair share of the profits, and you found it necessary to bilk her of what she was due."

Remington and Anderegg glanced at each other.

"I also know," Colbie continued, "you're responsible for Gregor Hoffer's murder. In case you didn't know, Gian Caflisch didn't have a problem spilling his guts to authorities about your illegitimate dealings. I suppose he figured he was destined for the lock-up anyway—why not take you down with him?"

Right then, Harold Remington thought it was a good time to shut his mouth. It was clear Colbie Colleen knew— she knew about Bachman's taking out Nicole and Fischer. She knew about Hoffer. She knew about the gun running.

In that moment, he realized she knew everything.

Anderegg, however, wasn't about to acquiesce. He stood, his massive frame meant to intimidate her. But, before he could say anything, Colbie caught him off guard. "I also know, Mr. Anderegg, you're the one who shot—and, killed— Reginald Champagne . . ."

Anderegg managed a disgusted look. "I killed him? You don't know what you're talking about—why would I?"

"Because he didn't like how things were going with the operation, and he threatened to shut it down." Colbie smiled. "You couldn't have that now, could you?"

"That's quite the story," Anderegg sputtered, raising his right arm with amazing speed, a silenced weapon pointed directly at Colbie. "You just couldn't keep your nose out of it, could you?"

"Why should I? Nicole hired me to find out who killed her brother, and I intend to make good on my contract."

Anderegg moved from behind his desk, the weapon trained on Colbie. "Get up!"

Colbie remained in her chair.

Christoph Anderegg wasn't used to being denied. "I told you to get up!"

Nothing.

Colbie merely smiled, further infuriating the bank's finest executive. "Tell me, Mr. Anderegg—am I right? Did you murder Reginald Champagne?"

Pistol still pointed at her, Anderegg's face blossomed with a brilliant flush. Harold watched, backing up against the wall, his cowardice on full display. He wasn't about to get involved in something destined to go south, and it didn't seem a good time to brandish his pistol.

Anderegg's voice dropped to a whisper. "You don't strike me as stupid, Ms. Colleen. If you don't want a bullet in your head, I suggest you do as I say . . ."

"Or, what, Mr. Anderegg?"

Anderegg ignored her impertinence. A woman treating him disrespectfully? Intolerable. Getting rid of Colbie Colleen would be a pleasure, even though it would probably be his last.

As Harold watched Anderegg sink further into a quagmire of deceit and murder, he recognized an opportunity that could, perhaps, extricate him from the current mess. At least, he hoped so—it was all he had. "That's a bunch of crap!" He looked at Colbie, then at Anderegg. "It's exactly as you say—he murdered Reginald Champagne so he can keep control of the arms operation!"

"Thank you for corroborating that, Harold. But, what about you? You seem eager to tell the truth, so why don't you tell me how you fit into the picture."

Harold squirmed, keeping his eyes focused on Anderegg—he was squirrelly enough to plug all of them. "All I did was initiate transactions . . . nothing else."

"And, Nicole?"

"She brought me business—that's all."

Colbie focused again on Anderegg, hoping Bollinger's backup was right outside the office door—an instantaneous vision told her things were about to go horribly wrong.

Upon hearing Remington's betrayal—well, it was all Christoph Anderegg could bear. Without a thought, he aimed the pistol at his long-time colleague and squeezed the trigger, only a momentary look of surprise on Harold's face. Remington slumped against his chair, one perfect bullet hole placed directly in the center of his forehead. Then, another.

He refocused on Colbie. "Stand up!" Anderegg's once booming, charming laugh morphed into a sneer.

Colbie didn't move.

That was it—Christoph Anderegg had enough.

Carefully, he aimed . . .

****

Bollinger placed his ear against Anderegg's office door. Nothing. Motioning to his officers, he took his stance to the side as an officer quietly turned the handle.

Still no sound from inside.

Weapon poised, the lieutenant carefully entered Anderegg's office, eyes strafing wall to wall—at first count, three bodies. Remington. Anderegg.

Colleen.

Blood spattered the wall behind Anderegg, a byproduct of blowing his brains out as Harold lay slumped against his chair, the double tap obvious. Colbie sat in her chair, blood trickling onto her right cheek.

"Get the medics in here—now!" There was no doubt Anderegg and Remington met their maker, but Colbie? A quick check of her wrist indicated a faint pulse. "Colbie?"

Nothing.

"Colbie . . . it's Bollinger. Can you hear me? If so, squeeze my hand . . ."

Nothing.

CHAPTER TWENTY-SEVEN

pril. May. June. Three months Colbie fought for her
life, slipping in and out of a coma as Brian remained
at her side, and Tammy took care of everything
stateside. Not talking about what could be an eventuality,
neither could envision their lives without her—both refused
to.

The fact Colbie was alive was a fluke. The bullet lodged
in the right side of her brain, a location that would, normally,
spell the end—that day, however, Anderegg was off his aim,
and the bullet skirted death's sweet spot. As time passed,
doctors offered little encouragement, gently preparing
Brian for the worst. "Chances are she'll never recover," the
neurologist commented while looking at her chart. "You
may have a decision to make sooner than later . . ." It was a
diagnosis Brian couldn't accept—in his gut, he knew Colbie
could beat the odds.

She had to.

Then, as their time in Zurich tipped in at one year, Colbie decided to step from her shadow world. No one knew she lay in its comfort, building strength through sheer desire, and only she would know the right time to emerge.

First, her left eye fluttered. "Colbie?" Brian leaned closer, taking her hand in his.

Then, both eyes opened, half-mast. "Brian?"

"Colbie!" Frantically, he pressed the nurse call button. "Colbie! I'm here!"

She moved her left hand slightly, its muscles weak from inattention. "Am I back?"

Tears spilled onto the collar of his shirt. "You're back . . ."

CHAPTER TWENTY-EIGHT

"Tammy!" Colbie hugged her assistant as soon as she walked through the door. "How's Chase? Is he happy at school?"

Tammy laughed, returning the gesture. "He loves it!" She paused as she dropped her car keys in her bag. "I can't believe you're back! Do you realize you were gone close to a year?"

Colbie laughed. "It doesn't seem possible, does it?"

"Well, I want to hear everything—and, don't leave anything out!"

"Then kick off your shoes, and get ready—it's a story you won't believe . . ."

As rain pelted the vintage windows of Colbie's and Brian's cottage, they took turns filling Tammy in on their months in Zurich—Harold Remington. Christoph Anderegg.

The eventual apprehension of Jan Bachman. "What started out as a relatively simple case, turned into multiple murders and intrigue . . ." Colbie stood as a cue to wind up the evening. "And, as you can imagine, Brian and I are exhausted! So—I'm kicking you out!"

Tammy grinned, grabbed her keys from her purse, and headed for the door. "You don't have to tell me twice!" She turned, looking fondly at her boss. "I'm really glad you're home . . ."

Moments later, she was out the door.

"We're so lucky to have her," Colbie commented as she picked up their wine glasses like she worked in a restaurant all her life.

"Indeed, we are . . ." He looked at Colbie, and patted the couch cushion. "Sit down . . ."

Colbie eyed him. "I need to get this stuff cleaned up . . ."

"You don't have to do that right now. C'mon—humor me. Come sit by me . . ."

She put down the glasses, then snuggled up against him. "Okay—I'm here!"

Brian squeezed her shoulders lightly. "Do you remember when we started this case, you said we could move back to the East Coast if we wanted?"

Colbie pulled back so she could get a good look at him. "Yes—is that what you want to do?"

"That's the thing—I don't think I do. Even though we've spent little time here, it feels like home. I never got that feeling when we were living outside of Boston."

Colbie sighed, finally allowing her body to relax. "I feel

the same way—back East, I never felt comfortable. It was like someone was always vying for my time, and I never had time to breathe."

Brian was quiet as he thought about their time away— his concern for Colbie's mental well being was still at the forefront of his mind, but he knew she'd get it together. "What do you think about asking the realtor if the landlord will sell us this place?"

"Live here? It's a little small . . ."

"True—but it's cozy. I kind of like that . . ."

They sat in comfortable silence for several minutes, thinking about starting over again. "Brian?" Colbie scooted closer to him.

"What?"

She paused to collect her thoughts. "I'm not sure I'm cut out to be an investigator anymore . . ."

"Why? You're just as good as you always were . . ."

Colbie shook her head. "Actually, I'm not. I'm beginning to think taking a bullet to the brain destroyed my ability to tune in . . ."

Brian thought for a moment. "Why do you say that? Have you tried?"

"Yes—and, there was nothing. And, it's happened more than once . . ."

That was a bombshell! He never considered her losing something important to the success of her business. "Maybe it's temporary . . ."

"Maybe—all I know is something is different. I can't be

as effective in my work if my intuition is on the fritz . . ."

Brian remained silent, then kissed her cheek. "If that's the case, all you have to do is approach your investigations differently—you know, like a normal person!"

Colbie belted out a gut laugh. "A normal person? What are you saying?"

"All I'm saying is your intuition isn't solely responsible for your success. Ever since I've know you, you've counted on it like it's an old friend . . ."

"But, it is—that's exactly what it's like!"

Brian looked at her, a comforting warmth in his eyes. "Your intuition doesn't define you—you define it." He paused, thinking about his own experiences with newfound abilities. "Besides—you always have me if your frequencies shut down!"

"That, I do!"

"Well . . . I suggest not giving it a second thought. You need time to deal with the trauma of a near-death experience—it's not something you can compartmentalize without understanding it."

Colbie knew he was right. She hadn't taken the time to give the experience its due—she didn't want to. "I don't know if I can do that," she admitted.

"You can—and, I believe once you do, your intuition will be back, full force. Maybe it will be stronger . . ."

"Until then?"

Brian grinned. "Until then we hang out in Aruba!"

"Aruba?" She thought about it for a moment. "I'm game!"

Brian wrapped both of his arms around her, resting his chin on the top of her head. "I love you, you know . . ."

"I know . . . and, I'm sorry."

Brian tilted her chin, allowing his lips to gently meet hers. "Apology accepted . . ."

PROFESSIONAL ACKNOWLEDGMENTS

CHRYSALIS PUBLISHING AUTHOR SERVICES
L.A. O'Neil, Editor
www.chrysalis-pub.com
chrysalispub@gmail.com

HIGH MOUNTAIN DESIGN
Wyatt Ilsley, Cover design
royaltywearllc@gmail.com